Gigi and Finn have a friendship that can't be broken—or that's what Gigi thought.

Gigi stared down at the two pizzas on the counter. There had never, *ever* been a time when she didn't know exactly where her best friend was. And she always knew because Finn *always* told her.

What was happening? Gigi wasn't sure, but she knew she didn't like it.

Before her mother could ask her what was wrong, she fled to her bedroom, closing the door firmly behind her. She half expected her mom to follow, but when she didn't, Gigi let herself have a good, long cry. Finley was her best friend. She had *always* been her best friend.

When Gigi had lost her first tooth and developed a somewhat irrational fear of the tooth fairy, Finn was the one who camped out in her bedroom and helped her keep watch. When Finn's beloved basset hound, Elvis, had passed away last year, it was Gigi who planned the funeral and cried with her for days. They rode their first roller coaster together, learned how to body surf together, got their ears pierced on the exact same day at the exact same time.

They had *history*. But did they have a future? For the first time ever, Gigi didn't know.

WITHDRAWN

PICTURE PERFECT

YOU

FIRST

Cari Simmons and
Lola Douglas

HARPER

An Imprint of HarperCollinsPublishers

For my momma

—L.D.

Picture Perfect: You First

Library of Congress Cataloging-in-Publication Data

Simmons, Cari, author.

You first / Cari Simmons & Lola Douglas.—First edition.

    pages cm.— (Picture Perfect ; #2)

Summary: When sixth-grader Gigi worries that her best friend Finn is
replacing her with her new friends on the soccer team, she thinks that their
friendship is over—but both girls learn that growing up means staying close
despite new interests.

ISBN 978-0-06-231058-3

[1. Friendship—Fiction. 2. Soccer—Fiction. 3. Middle schools—Fiction.
4. Schools—Fiction.] I. Douglas, Lola, author. II. Title.

PZ7.1.S55Yo 2015   2014022029

[Fic]—dc23   CIP

                                                                   AC

14 15 16 17 18   OPM   10 9 8 7 6 5 4 3 2 1

First Edition

"Can't you see it?" Gigi Prince asked her best friend, Finley. "Our name in LIGHTS!" Gigi held up her hands to show the giant theater-style marquee she pictured. It was Friday afternoon, and the girls were hanging out in Gigi's bedroom, waiting for the rain to pass. "What do you think?"

When Finn didn't answer right away, Gigi peered over the side of her loft bed. Finn was lying in the middle of a fluffy, grass-green carpet, doing crunches. These days, it was like she never *stopped* doing crunches.

"Finley!" Gigi said. "Our names. Lights. What do you think?"

"I think," she said between crunches, "that I need" (crunch) "a little more" (crunch) "information" (double crunch).

"Oh," Gigi said. "Broadway, of course. Or, more specifically, the Bright Lights of Broadway." As she said this, Gigi raised her hand and swept it in front of her, as if reaching towards the lights in the distance.

As an aspiring actress (and the lead in last year's elementary-school production of *The Cat in the Hat*), Gigi felt showbiz was in her bones. What could be a better party theme? They still hadn't decided on one, and they needed to—quick!

There were only six weeks left until the girls' twelfth birthdays, which Gigi found quite distressing. After all, it took *time* to plan the perfect double b-day celebration. Shopping for decorations, dreaming up favors, and even selecting the exact right thing to wear . . . none of that happened overnight.

"Think about it," Gigi continued, pulling her long auburn curls into an artfully messy knot on the top of her head. "We could get all glammed up, and play our favorite show tunes, and have one of those photo-booth stations with all kinds of crazy hats and props and stuff!"

Finn flopped backwards, putting her hands behind her head and wrinkling her nose. "I don't know, Gee," she said. "What would we be doing? Besides taking pictures?"

"Doing?" Gigi echoed. "Well, there'd be food. And cake, of course. Ooh! And we could play Celebrity."

"Celebrity?"

"It's this version of Charades, only everyone uses the names of celebrities," Gigi explained. "Julia Roberts swears by it."

Finley wasn't convinced. "What about that indoor rock-climbing gym?" she suggested. "That's cool and different, right?"

Now it was Gigi's turn to wrinkle her nose. "Different, yes. Cool? Depends on who you ask, I guess."

"I'm asking you."

"Then no."

Finley sat up, tucking her legs crisscross applesauce. "I just think we need to *do* something, you know? Like last year's party—the scavenger hunt at the mall. That was awesome."

She was right; it *was* pretty awesome. The two girls had recruited their mothers to help plan the event. The moms divided the girls and their guests into two teams, and they raced against each other across the mall, solving clues in the form of trivia questions about the birthday girls. At each stop, an employee of the store would hand off the next clue.

Gigi's team had won by a nose—or by a freckle, rather, since the final clue was this: "Finley has a freckle she named Fred. You'd go to this kiosk if you want to buy something for the body part on which Fred resides." (Answer: Piercing Pagoda). It was funny; Gigi hadn't so much as spoken a word about Fred since third grade, when the girls used to joke about the funny things the freckle would "whisper" in Finn's ear if she didn't feed him enough beef jerky.

Gigi reached behind her to grab Glamour Puss, which is what Finn had named the fluffy white kitty they'd made for her at Build-A-Bear. She hugged her favorite stuffed friend to her chest, trying to think of a party theme that represented both her and Finn equally. The task was harder than it sounded. Even though the two girls had been best friends since birth (earlier, actually, since their moms became BFFs when they met through a group for pregnant ladies), the truth was that things were changing. Things had *been* changing ever since they started sixth grade. At first, it was little stuff, like what Finn said when Gigi suggested they celebrate the first day of middle school with a mani-pedi ("Dude, do I look like I care about polishing my toenails?").

That was another thing—how "dude" had become Finley's favorite way of addressing people. (Gigi's response: "Dude? Do I look like I work on a ranch?")

Lately, though, Gigi felt as if the thin divide between them was beginning to widen. For example, she couldn't imagine ever wanting to spend a rainy Friday afternoon perfecting power squats. And as for Finley . . . well, she seemed completely uninterested in planning this party, when it was the *only* thing on Gigi's mind.

Gigi placed Glamour Puss gently against her pillow, then climbed down from the loft bed. She jumped two rungs from the bottom and landed with a thud. "Come on, Eff," she coaxed. "Can't you at least pretend to care?"

Finley paused, midcrunch, and frowned. "I *do* care, Gee."

"Really? Because you seem way more into what *you're* doing than what we're supposed to be doing together."

Finn sprang up to her feet and said, "You're right. I'm sorry. I'm just really excited about next week."

And this, perhaps, had been the biggest change of all. Because "next week" was the thing that Gigi was the *least* excited about. Next week was when the girls would be starting practice for the Sterling Middle School soccer team.

It wasn't that Gigi hated soccer. In fact, when they had first started playing, the summer after third grade, it had been *her* idea. She and Finley were obsessed with Harry Potter at the time. Of course, it wasn't possible for Muggles like themselves to join an actual Quidditch team, so at her dad's suggestion, she landed on the next best thing: an intramural soccer league.

Only soccer wasn't nearly as fun as she'd imagined Quidditch to be. There was all the *running*, for one thing. For another, it was too hot to wear her Gryffindor scarf during games. Before long, Gigi just grew bored.

Finley, on the other hand, loved soccer. Like, *really* loved it. She was fast on her feet and almost seemed to glide as she crossed the field. No one could match her in terms of passing—she was the best, plain and simple. Sometimes Gigi had more fun watching Finn play than actually playing herself.

Finn slipped a hair elastic off her wrist and pulled her shoulder-length blond hair into a low ponytail. "Okay," she said, narrowing her eyes. "Party planning. Let's do this."

Gigi couldn't help but laugh. Of course Finn would approach their task with the same intensity as a big soccer match. Of course she would.

"What we need," Finn continued, "is a strategy."

Gigi shook her head. "What we need is the Wall."

The two of them turned to face the wall opposite Gigi's loft bed. It was fourteen feet of history between them. Every last inch had been covered with posters, pictures, stickers, pages ripped from magazines—if you could stick it somewhere, the Wall was where it went.

Finley had actually started the tradition, with a picture of the two of them taken on the first day of preschool. They were dressed in matching blue jumpers and red-sequined flats, and they grinned at the camera, arms linked and heads touching. She'd pasted it smack in the center of the Wall, which at the time was covered with Disney princess wallpaper. Finn declared, "Princess Aurora, you are hereby banished from the Kingdom of Bedroom. Long live Eff and Gee!"

It was a ritual they continued to this day, "banishing" the things they'd outgrown, like the sparkly Polly Pocket decal and a poster of a certain boy band of brothers. Whatever replaced the "banished" item was proclaimed to be superior—the best, coolest, most Eff and Gee thing *ever*.

Sometimes the ceremonies were solemn, like when they'd come down with a serious case of Bieber fever. Other times, they were beyond silly, like when they took turns replacing the heads of My Little Ponies with those of their favorite celebrities. Like centaurs, but with famous people. (Together Eff and Gee had declared, "Long live the cen-stars!")

There was the photo of last year's *The Cat in the*

Hat—with Gigi in costume and makeup as the titular feline, and Finn decked out as Thing 1—pasted among souvenirs from every other play and talent show Gigi and Finn had ever been in.

Another section of the Wall was devoted entirely to Birthday Parties Past; each year, the girls cut the number of their age out of theme-appropriate scrapbook paper and pasted a picture of themselves from the party on top of it.

There was last year's mall scavenger hunt, of course. For their tenth birthday blowout, they'd thrown a retro roller skating party at the Christiana Skating Center. For nine, they both dressed up as Hermione Granger for their Harry Potter party, and two years before that was the karaoke slumber party they had in Finley's basement. They'd invited so many girls, you couldn't so much as walk to the bathroom without stepping on someone's sleeping bag.

Gigi's eyes rested on her favorite photo of the bunch—the superglam portrait of her and Finn from their sixth birthday party, which had been held at a Sweet & Sassy salon in neighboring Pennsylvania. Because of the distance, their parents had rented them an honest-to-goodness pink limo, and all of their best girlfriends piled in. The only grown-ups allowed were

Gigi's and Finley's moms. Technically, Finley's little brother, Logan, had been on board too, as he'd hitched a ride in Finn's mother's swollen belly.

"Remember how much fun that was?" Gigi asked, running her finger along the photo's glittery pink frame.

"Aww," Finn cooed. "Look how cute we are in those matching sequined tutus!"

"Whatever we decide for this party," Gigi said, "I feel strongly that it should include costumes."

Finn sighed. "Not everyone likes to play dress-up, Gee."

"But *we* do," Gigi responded. "And it's *our* birthday. So. If our friends want to bask in our fabulousness, they're going to have to dress appropriately."

Finley nodded like she agreed but then started to nibble on an invisible hangnail on her thumb. This, Gigi knew, was something her best friend did when she was conflicted. A nervous habit, born out of the fact that Finn hated to argue about anything.

Now it was Gigi's turn to sigh. Why wouldn't Finley just talk to her? How hard was it to tell your best friend what you were really thinking?

Then, as if she had read Gigi's mind, Finley said, "It's just that . . . well, costumes are more *your* thing than mine. So couldn't we, um, make them optional?"

"Of course," Gigi said. "As long as they stay on the menu. Deal?"

Finley grinned. "Deal."

The girls continued to bat ideas back and forth. Or rather, Gigi batted ideas to Finn, who proceeded to shoot them down.

GEE: What about a Southern tea party? We could have finger sandwiches and—ooh!—I can ask my mom-mom to make her famous seven-layer coconut cake!

EFF: Tea party? I thought we were turning twelve, not a hundred and twelve.

GEE: (Thinking.)

EFF: (Staring at same invisible hangnail.)

GEE: I know! We can go full-on Peter Pan, complete with pirate treasure hunt.

EFF: (Shoots Gee a look.)

GEE: What? You wanted something younger!

EFF: Maybe not that young.

GEE: Okayyy. How about a supercool Las Vegas theme? We could play poker—with M&Ms, of course.

EFF: Of course.

GEE: It could be really swanky. Ooh! We can

make the invitations out of playing cards!

EFF: Huh.

GEE: What?

EFF: *Southern tea?* Steel Magnolias. *Peter Pan?*
Hook. *Vegas?* Ocean's Eleven. *Do you
have any birthday party ideas not inspired
by a Julia Roberts movie?*

GEE: *What's wrong with Julia Roberts?*

EFF: *Nothing. I'm just saying, our party doesn't
have to have some kind of tie to your
redheaded spirit twin.*

[END BRAINSTORM SESSION]

Gigi flopped back on the carpet, covering her face with her arms. "This is hopeless!" she cried. "We're getting nowhere."

"True," Finn agreed. "You know what we need? A break."

"A break from what?"

"We're thinking way too hard about this. I say we go downstairs, make a couple of smoothies, and watch a movie. I'll even let you pick which one."

"Even if it's *Runaway*—"

"*Bride*," Finn finished for her. "Yes. I had a feeling you'd go for that one."

And just that like that, Gigi felt the party-planning tension melt clean away.

As the closing credits rolled, Finn put her sneakers back on and tightened the laces.

"Are you leaving?" Gigi asked.

"It'll be getting dark soon," Finley said. "I need to finish my run."

"But what about the party?"

"Tomorrow," Finn said. "After cooking class. I promise we'll figure it out then. 'Kay?"

Gigi nodded. She wasn't sure why she felt quite so deflated. It must've shown on her face, though, because Finn said, "Don't look so mopey. We'll get this party planned. We always do." Finn waved as she jogged out the door. "It's the weekend. We'll have plenty of time. Thank *god* it's Friday, right, dude?"

Finn headed out the door, and Gigi trudged back upstairs to her room.

It was just shy of five, which meant it was almost eleven in Prague. Her father's company had sent him there earlier in the week, but work had kept him so busy they'd only Skyped once, instead of every day like they usually did on his extended business trips.

At her desk, Gigi fired up her laptop. She launched

Skype and clicked to connect with GeorgePrince71, but he didn't answer. This is exactly why, she thought, her mother simply had to get her an iPhone for her birthday. That way she could just text her father, like any normal girl her age.

Disconnected from her dad. Ditched by her BFF. *TGIF?* Gigi thought. *Yeah, right.*

CHAPTER 2

When Gigi woke up the next morning, she thought, *Today is going to be the most excellent of days.*

The rain that had been graying up the world for practically a full week was gone, gone, gone. In its place was a butter-yellow sun and a sweet early spring breeze.

Gigi threw open her closet door and surveyed its contents. The weather had been too cold—not to mention too wet—to wear some of her favorite pieces. But today? Today was a day to bring out the wow. She fingered the ruffled hem of a purple-and-teal tie-dyed maxi dress that was so new, it still had the tags on it. She could pair the dress with a cardigan to make it more March friendly. There was also her pink ombré eyelet mini, the color of which made her think of a fluffy cloud of cotton candy. If she layered that over some white leggings, she might make it out of the house without her mother ordering her to change.

Then Gigi homed in on a navy-and-white-striped boatneck tee that screamed "classic nautical." She could wear it under the retro-looking denim overalls she had scored on sale at Forever 21. That was definitely more weather appropriate. Plus, they would look so boss with her cherry red Converse high-tops . . . or even her well-loved Sperrys.

And overalls *were* the most practical choice. After all, she and Finley were headed to cooking class, which often got messy.

Gigi wasn't the most careful chef. No matter what she was making, or in whose kitchen she was making it, the end result was always the same: walls spattered and countertops covered with a mix of ingredients. Baking was the worst; when Gigi made anything that included flour, she somehow managed to coat the entire kitchen in white.

So . . . which outfit? And considering the cooking class part of the day, did it really matter?

Time for a second opinion. Gigi looked at the clock. It was just after eight thirty, which meant she couldn't call Finn for another half hour (house rules). She added this to the list of reasons that both of them should be getting cell phones for their twelfth birthdays: being able to call each other at any time without disturbing the sleep schedules of other family members.

So far, her *top* argument—that everyone else got theirs for their *tenth* birthday—hadn't carried much weight with either set of parents. In fact, her mom was still insisting she wouldn't need a cell phone until she was sixteen! That was her mother, though. Stuck in the nineties.

"Good morning, sunshine!"

Gigi's mom greeted her cheerfully as Gigi entered the kitchen. She'd been hoping for a bowl of cereal and was surprised to find her mother squirting pancake batter over strips of cooked bacon on the griddle. Bacon pancake dippers were Gigi's absolute favorite, but they took a lot of time and effort to make. That's because in the Prince house, pancakes didn't come from a prepackaged mix, and it took forty minutes to roast the bacon alone. Typically, she had to beg her mom to make the dippers, and even then her request was only granted on birthdays and other superspecial occasions.

"What's the deal?" Gigi asked, looking to the stove. "Did I, like, get a really good report card or something?"

"You always get good report cards," her mother replied. "That's the reason we keep you around."

Gigi's eyes narrowed suspiciously. "True. But you never, ever make bacon pancake dippers for no reason."

"This is also true," her mom said, focusing hard on the pan. Almost as if she was avoiding looking at Gigi altogether.

"Spill," Gigi said, sliding onto a stool at the breakfast bar.

Her mother wiggled a thin orange spatula under one dipper and flipped it. Perfectly golden, of course. She made her way down the line, flipping each one with a kind of precision Gigi couldn't help but admire. It sounded cheesy, but her mom really was her culinary idol.

"Come on, Mama," Gigi said after a long silence. "Tell me what's going on."

"It's your dad," she said finally.

And just like that, Gigi knew. "He's not coming home tomorrow, is he?"

Her mom shook her head.

"How long this time?" Gigi asked.

"At least a week. Maybe more."

Gigi felt like a fallen soufflé. When her dad had taken this new job a year ago, they'd all known there would be more travel involved. *International* travel in particular, which Gigi thought was beyond cool. But lately it seemed like he was gone more than he was at home. Gigi didn't like that part one bit.

"I know you're disappointed," her mom said. "But your dad wanted me to let you know that the reason he's being delayed is because he has to go to Italy."

"Italy," Gigi repeated. "As in . . . *the* Italy?"

"Yes, my love. *The* Italy."

Gigi let out a tiny *squee*. Italy was number one on her list of dream destinations. It beat out Disney World by a mile. *Roman Holiday*, one of Gigi's favorite movies, was set there.

"Shoes," she said firmly. "Daddy definitely needs to get me some Italian shoes. From Italy."

"As opposed to Italian shoes from Denmark?" her mother teased.

Gigi fought the urge to roll her eyes, if only because it drove her mother crazy and she had that cell-phone campaign to wage.

Thinking of the campaign reminded her of last night's botched attempt to contact her father. "Hey, when did you talk to Dad?" she asked her mom. "I tried to Skype him last night, but he didn't pick up."

"He called early this morning. You were sound asleep, or I would've handed you the phone."

Gigi set aside her sadness long enough to say, "You

know, if I had an iPhone, I could just text him like a normal person."

"Or," her mom said, "you could just email him like a normal person. You do have that very nice laptop Mom-Mom got you for Christmas." With that, she slid her spatula under three dippers at once and placed them squarely on a small plate. "Here you go," she said, handing it over to Gigi. "Why don't you grab the maple syrup from the fridge?"

At exactly 9:01, after Gigi finished washing the last breakfast dish, she grabbed the cordless phone and bounded up the stairs to her room, keying in speed dial 3. Ms. Marian, Finn's mom, answered on the third ring.

"Hi, Ms. Marian," Gigi said. "May I please talk to Finley?"

"Finley's not here," Ms. Marian said. "She didn't call you?"

"Uh, no."

"She's spending the day at the Kirkwood Soccer Club," she said, "for a one-day boot camp. She was supposed to let you know, seeing as the two of you wouldn't be carpooling to your cooking class."

"Oh," Gigi said, caught off guard. "She . . . um . . . thanks for letting me know."

"Sweetie, I'm sorry," Ms. Marian said. "This was a last-minute decision. She didn't even know about the camp until last night. She was going to call. It must have slipped her mind."

"Oh . . . kay."

"I'll make sure she calls you back," she said.

"Okay," Gigi said again. "Thanks."

She pressed the off button on the phone, unsure of how she felt. She wasn't angry or anything like that. But something gnawed at the pit of her stomach.

Hurt, she realized. *I feel hurt.* After all, Finley had never skipped cooking class before. And she'd never, ever just blown Gigi off like that—without so much as a call.

Class didn't start until eleven, which meant she had more than an hour before she had to leave. So Gigi did the only thing that made sense to her: she climbed up the rungs to her loft bed, curled up with Glamour Puss, and pulled her comforter over both their heads.

CHAPTER 3

Gigi's mother found her lying in bed, flat on her back, staring blankly at the ceiling.

"Why aren't you dressed yet?" she asked. "We need to get a move on."

"I'm not going," Gigi informed her.

"Why not?"

Gigi shrugged, even though her mom probably couldn't see the movement under the blanket. "Don't feel like it."

"I repeat: why not?"

"Does it matter?"

"Gillian Gemma Prince!" Her mother let out an exasperated sigh. "Yes, it *does* matter. When my first and only child suddenly decides that she doesn't feel like going to the one thing she looks forward to all week long, I want to know why. Is this about your dad?"

"No."

"Then what?"

"It's Finley," Gigi confessed.

"Finley?" Her mother seemed confused. "Is everything okay? Did you girls get in a fight?"

Gigi paused, unsure how to answer. She and Finn weren't really *fighting*, but—

"Finn ditched me," Gigi said flatly. "She went to some daylong soccer boot camp. Didn't even bother to tell me."

"Well, that's . . . unfortunate. But why does that mean that *you* can't go to class?"

"I didn't say I couldn't," Gigi corrected her. "I said I didn't *feel* like it."

"I've heard enough," her mom said. "You're going to get up, you're going to get dressed, and I am going to drive you to your class. End of story."

"But—"

"No buts," she said firmly. "I understand that you and Finley like to act as if you're a single unit, but that's not always possible, now is it? I think this is a perfect opportunity for you to branch out on your own. Let's shake a leg."

Gigi knew that when her mother spoke to her this way, there was no sense in arguing. She was never going to win.

And so a very grumpy Gigi marched over to her dresser, pulled out a random pair of jeans, and threw on a baggy black T-shirt. She coiled her long, curly hair at the base of her neck and secured the makeshift bun with a hair elastic. She stuffed her feet into some moccasins, grabbed a lightweight hoodie from the closet, and stormed downstairs.

The drive to the Open Kitchen—the place where she and Finn had been taking cooking classes for the past eight months—was fairly short, less than fifteen minutes door to door. Gigi's mom chattered on about the errands she had to run, the radishes she was getting ready to plant in the backyard garden, and how she was long overdue for a haircut. Gigi didn't say a word in response.

"If you think you're punishing me with your silence, you're wrong," her mother said, smiling at her in the rearview mirror. "It's always nice to have someone listen to you, instead of waiting for their turn to talk."

They pulled into the bustling parking lot of the shopping center where the Open Kitchen was located, and Gigi felt a sharp pang in the pit of her stomach. Was it . . . nerves? That made no sense. She was a veteran of the class; the only person who'd been enrolled longer than she and Finley was that weird girl who always wore her hair in two high pigtails and carried a metal lunchbox for a purse. Plus, hello? Aside from acting, cooking was her *thing*. How many times had Chef Angela complimented her on her skills? You know, when she wasn't giving her grief for making such a hot mess. Every. Single. Week.

And yet there were definite butterflies thrashing in her belly as she walked through the front door. She scanned the room quickly, sizing up the situation. Even though the place was fairly full, the station where she and Finn almost always worked was empty, as if it had an invisible RESERVED sign on it. Feeling relieved, Gigi dropped her things on her usual stool and slipped her apron on over her head.

"Well, hello there, Miss Gigi!" Chef Angela said, beaming a wide, toothy smile in her direction. "Running a little late today, aren't you?"

"Sorry about that," Gigi said with a sheepish grin.

"Not a problem," she replied. "Where's your partner in crime? It's time to get started."

"She couldn't make it today."

"That's too bad," Chef Angela said, "because we are about to have some serious fun with fondant." She knocked her knuckles on the table to get the class's attention. "Listen up, kiddos! I need y'all to wash your hands and dry 'em real good. You're about to go elbows deep."

Gigi perked up instantly. She'd totally forgotten that they were moving on to decorating today. Classes at the Open Kitchen were organized in units of four to eight weeks, depending on what was being covered. The first month of this unit had been spent exclusively on baking. They'd only made one frosting so far, and even that was just a basic buttercream. *Bo-ring.*

But this? Fondant? This was going to be *awesome.*

At the sink, Gigi scrubbed her hands as diligently as a surgeon and rinsed them in water hot enough to turn her skin pink. Finley was going to be so bummed that she had missed this. It was okay, though. Gigi had already decided that she'd catch Finn up on everything they learned today. That way, when Finn returned to class next week, she wouldn't be behind.

Chef Angela handed Gigi a fresh paper towel to dry off. "Listen, missy," she said. "I'm counting on you to keep things clean today. Can't have this place lookin' like it got hit by a powdered-sugar blizzard, now can I?"

Gigi grinned. "I'll do my best."

She was still smiling as she turned to head back to her station. The smile faded when she saw who'd taken up the seat next to hers—the one that normally belonged to Finn.

It was Weird Girl.

"Hiya," Weird Girl said, waving at her. "Heard you tell Chef Angie that your BFF couldn't make it today, so I thought, *Hey, maybe I should go hang out with that Gigi Prince.*"

Gigi blinked.

Weird Girl continued. "I mean, you and Blondie always seem like you're having such a great time. I'd be totally jealous, but I try to never *ever* be jealous, because it's kind of a wasted emotion, ya know?"

"Angela," Gigi blurted.

"Huh?"

"Her name is Chef Angela. Not *Angie*."

Weird Girl tilted her head to one side, her dark caramel pigtails flouncing along. It made her look a little like a cocker spaniel. "You don't like me, do you?" she asked, not unkindly.

"What? I never said that."

"You kinda didn't have to," Weird Girl said, smiling. "Your body language speaks volumes."

Her directness threw Gigi off guard.

Then it hit her.

Weird Girl, she thought. *I've been in class with this*

person for months, and I never even bothered to learn her name.

"I'm sorry I made you feel like I don't like you," Gigi said, after a few beats. "Honestly, I don't even *know* you."

"Fair enough," Weird Girl said. "How about a do over? I'll go first. Hiya, my name is Miranda, and I'd like to be your friend."

Weird Gir—*Miranda* stuck out her right hand for Gigi to shake. Gigi hesitated, not out of rudeness, but because shaking Miranda's hand would mean that both of them would have to scrub up again. Instead, Gigi waved at her like Miranda had when she first approached the table.

"I'm Gigi," she said. "And I promise I would totally shake your hand if I hadn't just scrubbed mine raw."

An enormous grin spread across Miranda's face. "Excellent. Yes. Right on for germ-free friendship."

There was something so gleefully goofy about Miranda that Gigi couldn't help but giggle.

"I know," Miranda said. "I'm weird. But I'm a *good* weird. I promise."

Working alongside Miranda was different from working alongside Finley. For starters, Miranda almost *never* stopped talking—even when Chef Angela was giving instructions. But it was more than that. Finn often approached a new recipe with the same intensity she brought to wall-pass drills, whereas Miranda seemed way more easygoing. She also seemed to get over-the-top excited about . . . well, everything.

"Ohmigod, love!" she squealed when Chef Angela explained they'd be making fondant from mini-marshmallows. "Marshmallows! I mean, really. Who would've thought? Am I right?"

For flavoring, Miranda suggested anise, which she explained tasted like black jelly beans.

"Those are my favorite!" Gigi confessed. "Everyone else I know *hates* them."

"I will never understand that." Miranda shook her head. "Black jelly beans are the *best*."

The girls worked as a pair, sharing a glass bowl of melted marshmallow and taking turns mixing in a ton of powdered sugar. Gigi put in extra effort to keep the powdered sugar inside the bowl, instead of all over their station. It helped that Miranda shared a cool trick that involved using a flexible cutting board, curved around the inside of the mixing bowl, as a sort of slide to help guide the sugar in. Somehow Gigi still managed to sugar-powder her nose (and cheeks and forehead), but hey—it was progress.

They'd tried to make their fondant black, to match the beans, but the white of the marshmallows turned the whole sticky lump a moody, murky gray. Miranda declared it "Pretty!" It made Gigi think of angry storm clouds, but she could sort of see where Miranda was going with the whole pretty thing.

"This totally feels like a project we'd do in tactile arts class," Miranda said. "I think I'm going to talk to my teacher about adding it to the syllabus."

"Tactile arts?"

"Yeah, it's like art meant to be experienced through touch. Touching it is part of the art itself."

"You get to take a class on that?" Gigi asked. "Where do you go to school?"

"Fletcher Academy," she replied. "My mom's into progressive education. We don't even get real report cards with grades, just lots and lots of comments."

"No grades?" Gigi shook her head. "How do you know how well you're doing without any grades?"

"By reading the comments!"

Gigi shook her head. It was difficult for her to imagine a world without "real" report cards.

"How funny is it that we've seen each other a million Saturdays but never had an actual conversation before today?" Miranda remarked as they wrapped up their balls of fondant to take home. "You and Blondie kind of have this thing, like the two of you inhabit the same universe but no one else is allowed to visit. Anyway, I'm sort of glad she couldn't make it today."

"Her name is Finn. And you know what?" Gigi said. "I didn't mind it so much either."

As she said the words, Gigi realized she meant them. What had started off as a sad-sack Saturday had turned into something really special—and all because Finn had decided to ditch her.

Huh. How about that?

"All right, kiddos!" Chef Angela called out. "Before we finish up, I need to tell y'all something." She waited for the group to quiet down before continuing. "This spring, the Open Kitchen will be hosting its first-ever Kids-Only Ultimate Cupcake Bake-Off. And guess what? First prize is a year of free cooking classes, plus *five hundred dollars'* worth of high-quality tools every budding pastry chef needs. Oh, and did I mention that Chef Dana Herbert, local winner of the TV show *Next Great Baker*, will be our special celebrity judge? Even the Cake Boss loved him!"

The room fell completely quiet for about fifteen seconds. Then everyone started talking and asking all kinds of questions at once. Gigi scanned the room, trying to figure out who seemed the most excited, but she didn't have to look far. Miranda's face was lit up like Fourth of July fireworks . . . which was exactly how Gigi felt.

"We are going to crush this thing," Miranda said confidently. "Bet you anything first place comes down to one of us."

Gigi grinned. "I'll take that bet," she said. Then immediately she thought, *What about Finley?*

Her hand shot up. When Chef Angela called on her, she asked, "Are we allowed to work with a partner?"

"Good question," Chef Angela replied. "I think it would be okay, as long as the team agrees to split the prizes."

Problem solved! She and Finn could enter the contest together. The unstoppable Eff and Gee would surely win the grand prize!

"Great idea," Miranda said. "If you and I pair up, then we won't be each other's direct competition."

Gigi's stomach sunk to her knees. "Um, I was thinking I might pair up with Finley."

"Ohh," Miranda said. "Right. Of course." She shrugged. "That's cool. Now I can beat you fair and square."

Even though she was smiling, Gigi couldn't help but wonder if she'd hurt Miranda's feelings. She hadn't meant to. She honestly liked Miranda.

"It's just . . . well, Finn and I tend to do stuff like this together."

Miranda waved her off. "No worries. Really."

The girls finished packing up their stuff in silence. Miranda slipped her wrapped fondant ball into her metal lunchbox purse and snapped the latch shut. "Catch you later," she said.

CHAPTER 4

Gigi decided to put on her game face before sliding into the backseat of her mother's car. She wasn't ready to talk about what had just happened, partly because she had a feeling her mom wouldn't approve.

"Hey, sweetness," her mom said. "How was class?"

"Good."

Her mom laughed. "That doesn't sound very convincing."

"Oh," Gigi said. "Sorry. It was *really* good, actually." She quickly filled her mom in on the Kids-Only Ultimate Cupcake Bake-Off—leaving out the part about possibly hurting Miranda's feelings. Then she asked her mother if they could swing by the Brandywine Hundred Library before they headed home. She wanted to check out some cookbooks for inspiration.

On the short drive to the library, Gigi asked if Finley could spend the night, so that Gigi could fill her in on what she'd missed at class. "Plus," she added, "we're really behind on planning this year's party."

"I was hoping you and I could have a mother-daughter bonding night," her mom replied. "It's high time I introduced you to *Singin' in the Rain*."

"Yeah, but we can do that any night," Gigi said.

"I could say the same about having a sleepover with Finn," she pointed out.

Gigi was quiet for a minute. Then she said, "I call compromise."

"What kind of compromise?"

"We could do pizza and a movie—with Finley—and then make cupcakes inspired by the movie. I already have gray fondant and everything."

Her mother pulled into the library's parking lot. "That sounds fair," she said. "Let's pick up a pizza from Grotto's on our way home. A large cheese should be enough for the three of us, right?"

"Could we maybe get two, just in case?" Gigi asked. "That way, we'll have leftovers for breakfast tomorrow."

Cold pizza was her mother's favorite—a holdover, she said, from back in her college days. Gigi knew exactly what her mother would say before she even said it.

"Deal."

. . .

At home, Gigi pored over the cookbooks, looking for a cupcake flavor that would pair well with fondant that tasted like black jelly beans.

Gigi was so absorbed in what she was doing that she completely lost track of time. It wasn't until the light flooding the sunny kitchen had shifted that she even bothered looking at the clock.

Six, and she still hadn't heard from Finn.

Weird.

Gigi pressed 3 on the speed dial. This time, Finn's five-year-old brother, Logan, answered the phone.

"Hi, Logie," she said. "Can you get Finn on the phone?"

"No," he said.

Gigi was used to Logan saying "No." It had been his favorite word since he'd learned to speak.

"C'mon, Logan. I need to talk to your sister."

"Can't," he said. "She isn't home."

"Wait, what?"

"HOME," he said, louder this time. "SHE ISN'T HOME."

There was a bit of jostling, and then Gigi heard Ms. Marian wrestle the phone away from Logan. "Hello?" Ms. Marian said. "Who is this?"

"It's me, Ms. Marian," Gigi said. "I was calling for Finn, but Logie said she wasn't back from her boot camp yet."

"What? That ended hours ago. No, she's spending the night at a friend's house. Lauren?"

Gigi was stunned. *She* had plans with Finn tonight. And *Lauren*? *Who was Lauren*? There weren't any Laurens in their class.

Then it hit her: Lauren *Avila* was the eighth-grade co-captain of the varsity soccer team.

What was Finley doing hanging out with an eighth grader? That was, like, unheard of at Sterling Middle School. In fact, the eighth graders went out of their way to avoid lowly sixth graders.

"I—I didn't know," Gigi stammered. "She was supposed to call about our party."

"Oh, I am so sorry, Gigi!" Ms. Marian said. "I told her to talk to you and to apologize about skipping out on your class without offering an explanation. I don't know what's gotten into Finn lately. This isn't like her."

No, Gigi thought. *It really isn't.*

"That's okay," Gigi croaked.

Ms. Marian sighed. "I'm really, really sorry," she said. "I'll make sure she calls when she gets home tomorrow."

They said their good-byes just as Gigi's mom walked

into the kitchen. "Was that Finn?" she asked. "I am absolutely starving."

Gigi stared down at the two pizzas on the counter. There had never, *ever* been a time when she didn't know exactly where her best friend was. And she always knew because Finn *always* told her.

What is happening? Gigi wasn't sure, but she knew, whatever it was, she didn't like it.

Before her mother could ask her what was wrong, she fled to her bedroom, closing the door firmly behind her.

She half expected her mom to follow, but when she didn't, Gigi let herself have a good, long cry. Finley was her best friend. She had *always* been her best friend. When Gigi had lost her first tooth and developed a somewhat irrational fear of the tooth fairy, Finn was the one who had camped out in her bedroom and helped her keep watch.

When Finn's beloved basset hound, Elvis, had passed away last year, it was Gigi who had planned the funeral and cried with her for days.

They rode their first roller coaster together, learned how to bodysurf together, got their ears pierced on the exact same day at the exact same time. They had *history*.

But did they have a future?

For the first time ever, Gigi didn't know.

Eventually Gigi's tears ran dry. Her face had grown puffy, and she knew her sore eyes were rimmed in red without even looking in the mirror. But in a weird way, she felt better. She hugged Glamour Puss to her chest and took a few deep cleansing breaths.

There was a knock on her bedroom door, and for a split second, Gigi thought it might be Finley, home early from Lauren's because she felt so bad about ditching her.

But of course it was her mother instead. She poked her head through the doorway and asked, "Mind if I come in?"

"Sure."

Her mother flicked the switch, flooding the room with light. Gigi blinked rapidly, trying to adjust. When her eyes could focus, she saw her mom standing by her bed.

"I talked to Ms. Marian," she said.

Gigi gasped. "What? No! Why?"

"Because she's *my* best friend," her mom said. "And because I wanted to know what was going on."

Gigi sniffed. "What did she say?"

"That Finley was spending the night at someone else's house tonight."

Gigi nodded.

"But I figure there has to be something else going on too," her mother continued. "After all, it's not like you girls haven't had sleepovers with other friends before."

This was true.

"But . . . we always know about that stuff ahead of time. It's not, like, a secret when Finn goes to Katie's house, or when I spend the day with Kendall or whatever. This felt like, I don't know . . . hidden or something."

"Fair enough," her mom said. "So what do you think would help this situation?"

Gigi shrugged. "Pizza?"

"I meant with Finley."

She thought about her mother's question. She was pretty sure her mom had an answer already in mind. "Maybe you could save us both some time and tell me what *you* think I should do."

Her mom laughed. "Okay. I'm thinking that you need to put all of this out of your head tonight. We'll watch a movie, eat some pizza, bake some cupcakes. Then, tomorrow, you can let Finn know—nicely, of course—how you feel. I'd bet you anything that Finley has no idea that her actions would upset you, especially not this much."

Gigi wasn't entirely sure, but her mom was right about one thing: she couldn't resolve anything without talking to Finn.

"Vanilla almond," she said finally.

"What was that?"

"For the cupcakes," Gigi said. "I think vanilla almond would go really well with the anise-flavored fondant. Like those cookies we get at the Italian festival."

Her mother smiled. "Vanilla almond. Sounds like a plan."

CHAPTER 5

The next morning, Gigi's alarm went off at exactly 5:15 a.m. She shut it off without hitting the snooze button, even though she *really* wanted to go back to sleep.

Sunday morning before sunrise? No thank you.

Only she didn't have much of a choice—not if she wanted to surprise her mom with breakfast in bed. Both of her parents were early risers, even on the weekends. Not because they had to be, but because they genuinely liked getting up before the crack of dawn.

"Maximize your mornings," her dad always said. "Most people are at their best before eleven a.m."

When it came to her mother, productivity didn't seem to be a factor. "I just find it really peaceful," she'd say, holding a steaming mug of mint tea between her hands. "These are my moments of Zen."

Gigi rubbed at her hot, tired eyes and told herself to rally. There was sausage to be sizzled and French toast to be flipped. She wondered if they had any oranges left that she could use for fresh-squeezed juice.

The kitchen was where Gigi found her own Zen. It almost didn't matter what she was making; putting on her chef's coat immediately put her into the zone. She had a feeling that Miranda felt the same way, if how she acted in class was any indication.

Gigi finished off a fat stack of blueberry French toast by grating a little lemon zest on top. Her breakfast looked like something out of a magazine. She couldn't wait to see the look on her mother's face. She was in the zone, all right—so much so that she didn't even hear her mother enter the room.

"Aren't you a sweetie," her mom said, startling Gigi so much that she let out a horror-movie scream. The zester went flying behind her, smacking into the kitchen window with a loud *crack*.

"Holy wow, Mama!" Gigi exclaimed. "You scared me!"

"Sorry," she said. "I keep forgetting how quiet it is with just the two of us here."

Gigi pulled out two plates from the cabinet and fished a couple of forks out of the utensil drawer. "I was trying to surprise you."

"I can see that," her mom said. "And I'm very grateful."

They decided to eat in the dining room instead of the breakfast bar, to make the morning feel even more special. Gigi's mom took out two wineglasses and poured the juice into them. "Look at us," she said, "being all fancy."

Gigi speared a couple of blueberries on her fork. "I wanted to thank you for last night."

"What about last night?"

She gave her mom a knowing look. "I was sad, and then I wasn't. Because of you—and *Singin' in the Rain*. Just let me say thanks, okay?"

"Okay."

After breakfast, Gigi's mom insisted on doing the dishes. Gigi, uncharacteristically, insisted on drying.

The two stood side by side, listening to the soundtrack to *South Pacific* as they worked. Gigi's mother hummed along to "I'm Gonna Wash that Man Right Outa My Hair." Only instead of smiling, Gigi's mother looked terribly sad.

"You okay?" Gigi asked her.

"What? Yes, of course. I'm fine."

"You don't look fine," Gigi pointed out. "You look like someone kidnapped your dog."

Gigi's mother laughed. "Oh, Gee. You know your mama too well. To be honest, I was just thinking about

Daddy. I miss him so much, sometimes I feel like my heart is actually aching."

This caught Gigi by surprise. The past year had been rough on her, what with her father always getting on another plane. But her mom never seemed to mind all that much. Sure, she told Gigi's dad that she couldn't wait for him to get back, and she got extrahappy the day before he flew home. Other than that, though . . . sometimes Gigi wondered if her mom even realized her dad was gone.

"You're always so busy," she said. "I didn't know you had time to miss Dad."

"Why do you think I'm always so busy?" her mother countered. "Less time to think."

"Oh."

Gigi's mom shut off the faucet and dried her hands on a tea towel. "Before your dad took this job, we all talked about what it would be like, remember?"

Gigi nodded. Her dad had called a family meeting so that they could have a Big Important Conversation about it. He and her mom took turns pointing out all of the ways their lives would be different with her dad traveling sixty percent of the time. It made Gigi sad to think of her dad away for such long stretches, but when he listed some of the destinations—London, Paris, Madrid—well,

Gigi thought this new job couldn't sound any cooler.

But now that her mother mentioned it . . . it hadn't been until *after* her dad took this job that Mom had started teaching yoga twice a week, and volunteering at Dress for Success, this place that provided low-income women with suits and stuff for job interviews.

Over the past year, Gigi's mom had taken a lot of classes too—Investing in the Stock Market, Container Gardening, Conversational Spanish. And scrapbooking! Her mom had dabbled in it before, but now she was hard-core. Some nights Ms. Marian would come over with all of her gear and the two of them would take over the dining room, working on their albums for hours. She and Finley loved it, though; they'd camp out in front of the TV, watching movies until way past their normal weekend bedtime.

"You know," her mom said, "you could take a page out of my book."

"What do you mean?"

Her mother reached over and tucked some of Gigi's curls behind her ear. "The first few times Dad was away, I felt really sad, and even a little lonely. I tried not to show it, because I knew the transition was difficult for you. But when you weren't around, I was kind of a sad mopey."

"And?" Gigi said.

"And nobody likes to be around a sad mopey."

Just then, the phone rang. The robotic caller ID voice announced, "Call from Stewart, Ryan." Finley's dad. It was their house line. Her mom reached for the phone, but Gigi blurted out, "No, leave it!" She got a funny look in response.

"I'll call her back later," Gigi explained. "I want to finish our conversation."

Her mother nodded. "I'm going to put some water on for tea. Mint or chamomile?"

"Mint, please. So what happened then?"

"Ms. Marian happened," her mom replied. "She told me I had a choice. Either I could sit around feeling sorry for myself, or I could decide to take advantage of this extra time I suddenly had."

"So that's why you started taking all of those classes and stuff," Gigi said.

"Yep. And in the beginning, I would always think how great it would be if your dad were here to take some of these classes with me. Only I wasn't taking the kinds of classes that would interest your father. And in some ways, that was the best part."

"What do you mean?"

"When you're a wife and a mom, sometimes you can forget that you have interests outside of your family," her mom explained. "Ms. Marian reminded me of some of mine. It's kind of like getting to know myself all over again. And you know what? I'm pretty amazing."

"Not to mention humble," Gigi quipped.

Her mother poked her in the rib cage.

They took their tea into the living room and curled up on the couch, Gigi on one end and her mom on the other. She hated to admit it, but what her mother said made perfect sense. Almost everything she was involved in—no, scratch that, *everything* she was involved in—Finley was involved in, too. Cooking class, soccer, drama club . . .

And just like that, Gigi knew exactly what she had to do.

She started by making a list in the purple composition book that served as her sometimes diary.

Knitting
French Club
Play clarinet
Fencing
Go horseback riding
Volunteer at pet shelter
School newspaper

It was an ambitious list—especially the part about fencing. (Did they even offer fencing classes in Delaware? She'd have to do some research.) But at one time or another, Gigi had wanted to do all of the things on it, and Finn hadn't.

Well, that wasn't entirely true. They'd never discussed volunteering at a pet shelter before, but so much of Gigi's list was *me, me, me*. Her mom was a big believer in giving back to the community. Therefore, the pet shelter.

Gigi copied the list on a separate piece of paper, in her neatest handwriting. Then she went downstairs and handed it over to her mom. "Don't make fun, okay?"

"I would never," her mother assured her. She watched her mom's face as she read the list. It revealed nothing.

"So?" Gigi prompted.

"So, this is good," her mom said. "Although I didn't know you had any interest in pet shelters."

Gigi's cheeks pinked. "I didn't either. But now I think it sounds like a really great idea. So what's next?"

Her mother shrugged. "That, my dear daughter, is entirely up to *you*."

CHAPTER 6

Monday morning, when Gigi got on the bus, she was both relieved and nervous to see Finley sitting in their usual seat. She took a deep breath, walked to the back of the bus, and sat down beside her best friend.

"Hey," Finn said.

"Hey," Gigi said back.

Silence.

After a few minutes, Finn said quietly, "You must be really mad at me, huh?"

"Why do you say that?"

"Because you never called me back."

"Actually, I was planning on returning your call tomorrow," Gigi said smoothly. "Since, you know, that's how long it took you to call me to begin with."

Finley sighed. "So you *are* mad."

Duh, Gigi wanted to say. But she didn't.

Instead she said, "I was just kidding. It's fine.

Everything's fine." She punctuated that last sentence with a smile, waiting for Finley to call shenanigans.

Only . . . she didn't. Gigi had just bald-faced lied to her best friend in the entire world, and her best friend didn't even notice. Worse, she looked *relieved*.

"I was hoping you'd say that," Finn said. "And I'm sorry I didn't call you back right away. Everything just happened so fast." She proceeded to spend the rest of the bus ride talking about how fabulous the soccer boot camp was and how afterwards, Lauren invited a couple of girls to spend the night. "It was kind of cool, you know? Being the only sixth grader she included."

As much as Gigi hated to admit it, she could sort of understand why Finn did what she did. If the situation had been reversed—if Gigi had been the one invited to an eighth-grade sleepover—she might have made the same choice.

"So, um, I made a new friend too," Gigi said. "This girl at class. The one with lunchbox purse? Her name is Miranda."

"*Weird Girl?* The one with the pigtails?"

"Yes," Gigi said, feeling annoyed. "The one with the pigtails. She's awesome."

Finn smiled, but it didn't feel like a happy smile. It felt more like an uncomfortable one.

"Anyway," Gigi continued, "you missed a lot in class." She filled her in on the marshmallow fondant and the cupcake bake-off. Then she said, "The best part is that Chef Angela said we could work as a team, as long as we agreed to split the prizes. I'm thinking you can have the free classes, and I'll take the tool kit."

Finley's eyebrows furrowed, and she immediately began nibbling on her thumb's cuticle. *Uh-oh*, Gigi thought.

"You could have the tool kit instead," she said hurriedly. "Whatever you want."

"It's not that," Finn said. "It's just—"

"What?"

Finn shook her head. "Nothing. Never mind."

But Gigi knew it wasn't nothing. If Finley chewed on that cuticle any harder, she was going to draw blood.

"Something's bothering you," Gigi said. "Spill."

Finn blinked at her a few times, then said, "That boot camp I went to? It was sort of a tryout for this intense workshop. Coach said I could join, if I wanted to. But that would mean—"

"Giving up your Saturdays," Gigi finished for her. "For how long?"

"The whole spring. Probably summer too."

"Oh."

"But I haven't decided if I'm doing it yet," Finley blurted out. "I'm just . . . thinking about it."

"Oh," Gigi said again.

Finn cut her eyes down to the backpack resting in her lap. "The thing is, it's a really good opportunity. I mean, the sessions are hard—Lauren calls them 'punishing.' But this is her fourth year, and she swears the workshop is the only reason she made varsity as a sixth grader. Dude, that almost *never* happens."

"Wow."

Finn started up a steady stream of nervous chatter. But as she spoke, Gigi could feel the divide between them getting wider and wider. And the more Finn went on and on about Lauren—She was so athletic! And smart! And funny!—the more Gigi's brain got carried away with itself.

Lauren, Lauren, Lauren, said a mean little voice inside her. *What's the big deal about her?*

But Gigi knew what the big deal was. Lauren was an eighth grader, and super, *super* popular. There wasn't a kid in school who wouldn't want to hang out with her.

In homeroom, Gigi kept conversation to a minimum. She told Finn she needed to finish up some homework before French. Another lie. Instead she pulled the purple composition book out of her bag and opened it to her list. She added:

Find a new best friend?

Gigi stared at the words, trying to fight the hot tears that pricked up in her eyes.

No! She refused to cry. Because it couldn't be true. There was no, *no* way Finn could be looking to trade her in.

Even if it was for someone cooler. And older. And on the varsity team.

She turned to a fresh page and wrote:

I refuse to be a sad mopey.

Gigi forced the corners of her lips up into a smile, hoping her mouth could trick the rest of her into feeling happier.

At lunch, Finn plopped her tray down on the table she and Gigi shared with their friends Katie, Kendall, and Maggie.

Gigi tried to be lighthearted. "Oh! You're not having lunch with Lauren?" she joked.

"Don't be silly," Finn said.

Gigi was about to laugh when Finn added, "She's got B lunch."

Gigi swallowed a gulp of water.

"Who's Lauren?" Kendall asked, licking yogurt from a plastic spoon.

"Just this girl on the soccer team," Finn replied with a shrug. "We hung out last weekend."

Maggie said, "Isn't she in eighth grade?"

Finn nodded.

"Ooh! If you're hanging out with eighth graders, does that mean we'll start getting invited to eighth-grade parties?" Maggie asked.

Finley rolled her eyes. "In our dreams. Speaking of parties," she said, "Gigi and I are having a hard time coming up with a theme for ours. Any ideas?"

"That's right!" Katie cheered. "We're due for another Eff and Gee blowout!"

The girls spent the rest of the lunch period making a list of potential themes. Kendall suggested a Hawaiian luau. "But that's what we did for *your* birthday party," Gigi said.

Kendall shrugged. "So? You had fun, didn't you?"

Eff and Gee's eyes met. *Typical Kendall.* If it was great once, it would be great a hundred times. Like last summer, when she wore out her iPod playing that one Katy Perry song over and over and *over*.

"Ooh, I know!" Maggie said. "You should have one

of those murder mystery parties. Then you'll have to invite some boys."

The girls shook their heads no.

"Seriously?" Maggie said. "No boys?"

"Nope," Finn said.

"And no costumes." Gee followed a second later.

Maggie's jaw dropped. "No *costumes*? You've got to be kidding me!"

"Calm down, Mags," Gigi said. "Costumes are considered—"

"Optional," Finn finished for her.

"Optional." Maggie raised one eyebrow. "You guys are acting totally weird. You know that, right?"

Gigi broke the awkward silence that followed by handing out her vanilla almond cupcakes with anise-flavored fondant to her friends.

Kendall sniffed at the top suspiciously. "This smells like black jelly beans," she said.

"Just try it," Gigi said.

With her face screwed up like she'd already tasted something nasty, Kendall flicked out her tongue and ran it over the corner of the fondant.

"Are these . . . gray?" Katie asked.

"Dudes, don't be rude," Finn admonished them.

"Gigi baked for us!" She peeled the paper wrapper from the cupcake's base and, as if in defiance, crammed the entire thing into her mouth. "Mmm," she mumbled as she chewed. "Thish ish ood. Nice job, Gee."

"Thanks," Gigi said, smiling. There was the Finn she knew—always on her team.

Finley washed the rest of her cupcake down with a long swig of milk, then said, "We still don't have a party theme." She turned to Katie. "What about you? Any ideas?"

"Yes," Katie said, nibbling daintily on her dessert. "Purple."

"Purple?" Finn echoed.

"Purple," Katie said firmly.

"Purple is not a theme!" Gigi laughed. "Purple is a *color.*" The bell rang, signaling the end of lunch. As the cafeteria started to empty out, Finn tugged on Gigi's sleeve.

"I was thinking," she said. "Let's get together at your place Saturday afternoon to work on party stuff. We'll figure out this theme thing once and for all."

"Really?" Gigi asked. "Are you sure you won't have . . . *plans?*"

"It was *one* sleepover, Gee," Finn said, gently

nudging her with her elbow. "Don't make such a big deal out of it, okay?"

As she headed to her next class, Gigi thought about what Finn said.

Maybe she *had* been making a big deal out of nothing. After all, she and Finn had nearly twelve years of friendship between them. Lauren Avila? Didn't even have twelve days.

For the first time all day, Gigi didn't have to force herself to smile.

CHAPTER 7

Six laps. Coach made them run six laps. As a warm-up.

Despite the cool weather, Gigi's face was damp with sweat as she completed the final circle around the field.

"Pick up the pace, Princess!" Coach called out to her.

Gigi glared at her as she jogged a little bit faster. She was pretty sure that Coach Wedderburn didn't like her very much. Finn said that was just Coach's personality—that she was all business and no fluff. But Gigi knew better. The first day of tryouts, when Gigi showed up in her new hot-pink cleats, Coach called her out.

"Pink, huh?" she said. "*Pretty*. Like a princess."

It might have been meant as a compliment. Except it didn't sound like one to Gigi. Every other girl at tryouts had opted for plain black cleats. What was wrong with having a little style?

"It's the uniforms," Finley explained afterwards. "They're red and black. Pink cleats . . ."

"Totally clash." Gigi finished for her. "I am an idiot."

"You are unique," Finn said. "Besides, if anyone could pull off that color combo, it's you, dude."

"Hustle, Gigi!" Coach said. "We're all waiting for you."

Why did I pick this? she thought as she pounded out the last hundred yards. *Why am I torturing myself?*

Coach blew her whistle, even though the entire team was already standing in front of her. "All right, Songbirds. Today we're going to work on team building. How many of you have done bounce bounce pass drills?"

Only one hand shot up: Finley's.

"Stewart, front and center." Coach tossed her clipboard on the ground, near Gigi's pink cleats, and traded it out for a slightly muddied soccer ball. "The way the bounce bounce pass works is that you bounce the ball to yourself twice, like this." She dropped the ball, catching it on her right ankle. After balancing it, she popped the ball back up and caught it on her left. "After you've bounced to each ankle," she continued, "you're going to pass the ball to your partner." Coach shot the ball in Finn's direction.

Finn expertly bounced the ball onto one ankle, then the other, before cleanly kicking the ball back to Coach.

"Nice work, Stewart," Coach said with clear admiration. "Where'd you learn that?"

"Coach Campbell. I'm taking her weekend workshop."

Coach nodded. "I approve."

Next, Coach split the team into partners. There were other girls on JV who, like Gigi, were nowhere near Finley in terms of skill. But for some reason, Coach paired Gigi with Kionna, a strong, sturdy girl who had at least six inches on her. Gigi knew Ki, as she liked to be called, was good—way better than Gigi could ever hope to be.

"You don't need to look so scared," Ki said. "I'll go easy on you."

Ki went first. Her bounces weren't as clean as Finn's or Coach's, but she could do them. When she passed the ball to Gigi, she did so with such force that it sailed over Gigi's head and landed a hundred feet down the pitch.

Gigi turned to look at the ball. Ki started cracking up.

"I'm just messing with you," she said as she jogged past Gigi to retrieve the ball and dribble it back. Then she passed the ball to Gigi. "Your turn," she said.

Gigi swallowed hard. She tried to repeat the move. Her first bounce, on the right ankle, was a success. The second? Not so much.

They continued to take turns, Ki nailing the move and Gigi floundering through several unsuccessful attempts. Eventually Gigi completed her bounce bounce pass.

"I did it!" she said. "I actually did it!"

Gigi didn't have any time to savor the victory, though, because Ki was so quick, the ball was already headed back her way.

This time Gigi executed the move more fluidly. The girls spent the next few minutes passing the ball back and forth between them. Gigi was so hyperfocused on the drill that she didn't notice when Coach approached them.

"Good job, Johnson," Coach declared as Ki sent the ball Gigi's way. Coach's gravelly voice startled her so much that Gigi let the ball sail right by her.

With her eyes still trained on Gigi, Coach lifted her whistle and gave it a short, hard blow. "All right, team!" she said. "Time to get back to basics. We're going to spend the rest of today's practice working on dribbling and turning. Stay with your partners, ladies—but make sure one of you grabs a pinny."

"Not it!" Ki called out, touching two fingers to her nose. She grinned at Gigi and pointed to the mesh bag that held the scrimmage vests.

Gigi trudged over to the bag and fished one out. Finn jogged up and joined her. "Hand me one?" she asked.

Gigi held the pinny up to her nose and breathed in. "Is it me, or do these smell like twenty-year-old sweat?"

"Nah," Sunny Nguyen, a seventh grader, said, pulling hers on over her head. "Coach washes them weekly."

The pinnies were a particularly disgusting shade of mustard yellow, and no matter what Sunny said, they had a distinctive smell. Oddly enough, it reminded Gigi of hot dogs.

She turned to say as much to Finley, but she was already gone.

For the last fifteen minutes of practice, Coach divided the girls into two teams of seven: pinnies versus non-pinnies. At least she and Finn were on the same team.

Not surprisingly, Coach made Finley the left

forward. Finley always played forward. She was fast, she was fierce, and she scored points.

Then Coach went ahead and made Gigi the *right* forward.

Gigi was stunned. She had never been a forward before. Her other coaches had always buried her somewhere less important.

"You sure about that, Coach?" Finn called out. "Princess usually plays midfield."

Gigi's cheeks burned. Finn of all people knew how much the Princess nickname bothered her. Did her *supposed* best friend really just call her that? In front of everyone?

"I wouldn't have said it if I wasn't sure," Coach shot back.

Finn apologized, Coach finished calling positions, and Gigi thought, *Oh, it's* on.

The whistle blew.

Gigi went straight for the ball, but Finley reached it first. Of course she did. As the defensive line closed in on Finn, Gigi waited for the pass.

It never came.

Instead, when she couldn't get any farther down the pitch, Finn took a strong but long-shot kick to the goal.

The lanky sixth grader playing goalie caught it so easily, she looked completely startled. Coach blew the whistle.

"What was that, Stewart?" she yelled. "I know Coach Campbell didn't teach you to be a ball hog. You should've passed to Princess."

Princess. Gigi fumed. She was nobody's Princess. She was Gigi Prince, and she was about to throw down.

Gigi's eyes stayed trained on the ball. When Kionna attempted to pass to a particularly spacey teammate, Gigi intercepted. She'd already dribbled the ball halfway to the goal before anyone even realized she had it. She had two options for passing: Finley or Sunny. She chose Sunny.

The two girls moved closer to the goal, but Gigi had the better shot, so Sunny passed the ball back to her. With one strong kick, Gigi scored her very first goal.

Her mouth dropped open in disbelief. So did Finley's.

"Nice work!" Coach called out. "See, Stewart? Now *that's* how it's done."

Play continued, and while Eff and Gee were technically on the same team, to anyone watching, the scrimmage looked like it was full-on Princess versus Stewart. And, for once in their soccer careers, it was Gigi who was dominating.

"Princess, you are on *fire!*" Coach hollered.

"Then stop calling me Princess!" she shot back.

Coach chuckled.

The two-minute warning was issued. Gigi thought how sweet it would be to score one last goal. She ran down the pitch, determined to do just that. From the corner of her eye, she saw Finley horn in on her path. Gigi let out a weird, guttural sound, like she was suddenly an extra in some movie with gladiators, and pushed her pace even faster.

And then her heel struck a mushy patch of grass, and she went flying backwards.

Rrrrrripppppp.

Gigi landed on her butt with a dull thud. Her tailbone screamed in pain. When she slipped her hands under her to rub it, she realized that her cute Nike Pro shorts had ripped straight up the back seam.

Coach jogged over to her. "You okay, Prince?" she asked.

Gigi smiled despite the pain and future humiliation of having to cross the field with her undies showing. "You didn't call me Princess!"

"You're fine," Coach declared. "All right, team. See you next practice. Work on your dribbling before Wednesday."

Gigi didn't move.

Kionna appeared, thrusting a hand in Gigi's direction. "Take it," she commanded.

"Um, thanks, but I think I need a few minutes."

Ki shook her head. "Whatevs."

Gigi stayed as still as possible, hoping no one else would offer to help. Her plan was to wait out the team before heading in to change. That way she could (theoretically) minimize the undie peeping.

No such luck.

Finn stood over her, hands on her hips. "You ripped your shorts, didn't you?"

"Why do you care?" Gigi shot back.

"Seriously?" Finn asked. "Dude, you're my best friend—even when you act like a brat."

Gigi sprung to her feet, ignoring the burning pain in her backside. "First of all," she said, "stop calling everyone dude. It's annoying. We're girls, remember? And don't you ever—EVER—refer to me as Princess again, to anyone. It's insulting. And finally, I can't believe you'd say that *I* was acting like a brat. Why is that? Because I dared to score a goal? *You* were the ball hog, remember? I just happened to not suck for one practice."

With that, she turned on her heel and stormed off

towards the locker rooms. Finley followed her closely. Too closely, actually. Gigi stopped short, and Finn ran right smack into her. She whirled around to face her, but Finn stayed close behind no matter what direction she turned.

"What are you *doing*?" she asked angrily.

"I," Finn said, "am trying to make sure no one sees your Monday undies."

In her spurt of sudden rage, Gigi had practically forgotten about the enormous rip in her shorts. "Thanks," she muttered, feeling far more grateful than she sounded.

After they'd changed out of their practice clothes, Finley said, "I'm sorry about the Princess comment. I was—"

"Showing off?" Gigi finished for her.

Finn's cheeks flushed a hot pinky-red. "Maybe. Not on purpose, though."

"Okay. Thanks."

"And you don't suck," Finn added softly.

Gigi didn't respond directly. She didn't know how to feel.

On the one hand, Finley had acted like a first-class jerk. On the other, she'd had Gigi's back, literally, when she was in an embarrassing spot.

When did their friendship get so . . . *complicated*?

Gigi stuffed her cleats in her bag and said, "I think my mom's got carpool today. Meet you out front?"

She walked away before Finn could even respond.

CHAPTER 8

Later that night, just as Gigi and her mom sat down to a yummy chopped barbecue chicken salad that was a favorite of Gigi's dad, the phone rang. The caller ID voice announced Finley's house line, but Gigi didn't move.

"Aren't you going to beg me to get that?" her mom asked.

"No."

Gigi liked preparing her father's favorite dishes when he was gone, because it helped her feel like he wasn't quite so absent. She stabbed the perfect bite of salad—romaine lettuce, grilled chicken, red onion, fresh nectarine, and homemade barbecue dressing—and continued to eat. The phone rang three more times before going to voice mail. Her mother simply stared at her.

When Gigi realized her mom wasn't going to let this go, she put down her fork and said, "Finn acted like a jerk today at practice. She apologized, but . . ."

"What happened?"

Gigi told her mom all of the humiliating details. But her mother, being her mother, focused on all the wrong things.

"Do you feel like your coach is being too hard on you? Because I can call the school and—"

"No!" Gigi said sharply. "She was just being Coach, okay?"

They ate without speaking. Quiet dinners weren't the norm in the Prince household. Her mother, a big believer in families eating together, insisted on leisurely meals filled with conversation.

Thankfully, her mother broke through the unnatural silence. "Oh!" she said. "I almost forgot. The Chinese American Community Center offers youth fencing classes. The next session doesn't start for a few weeks, but they're holding a sample class this Sunday. I signed you up—hope that's okay."

"Seriously?" Gigi said. "That's so excellent! Mama, you are the *best*." She jumped up from the table to give her mom a hug. "So," Gigi said, after returning to her seat, "did you book any other classes for me?"

"Nope," her mom said. "After all, it's *your* list. You need to put in the work yourself."

•••

After doing the dinner dishes, Gigi went up to her room and set up shop at her desk. She had some geography homework to tackle, but before she dove into that, she figured she better make some progress on her list.

It didn't take long for her to find what she needed. A quick Google search revealed that the Brandywine Hundred Library offered Purl Jam, a weekly knitting club, on Thursday nights. She didn't bother to look any further because between that, soccer practice, cooking class, and the fencing thing, Gigi figured her week was already overloaded. Plus, she still had a cupcake bake-off to prepare for, and tryouts for the spring musical were fast approaching. Gigi was eager to get started on her audition piece, but her drama teacher, Mrs. Dempsey, had yet to announce this year's show.

Gigi had just cracked open her geography text when there was a knock on the door. It was her mom, offering her the phone. "Someone wants to speak to you," she said.

Finn. Gigi scowled but took the receiver. "Hey," she said flatly.

"How's my favorite girl?" her dad asked, his voice as rich as a double-fudge chocolate brownie.

"Daddy!" she cried. "You have *no idea* how much I miss you."

"I think I do," he said. "But go on and tell me anyway."

They chatted for the next ten minutes or so. Gigi filled her father in on the good-parts version of her life. She'd gotten to speak to him so infrequently lately that she didn't want to waste precious minutes dwelling on the not-so-hot stuff. For instance, she told him about making friends with Miranda but decided not to share Coach's annoying nickname for her.

She tired of talking about herself rather quickly. "Tell me about Italy," Gigi begged her father. "Don't leave out a single fabulous detail."

She grilled him about the food, the fashion, the art. He gave her a play-by-play of his hotel and told her the pasta he'd had so far was "pretty tasty."

"Seriously?" she said. "That's all you're going to give me?"

Her dad chuckled. "You do realize I'm here on business, right?"

Gigi started to protest, but her father let out an enormous yawn. "Sorry, honey," he said. "It's a little late here. I'm totes exhausted." She'd forgotten about the six-hour time difference; a quick glance at the clock revealed that, for her dad, it was almost one in the morning.

"Don't say 'totes,'" Gigi said.

"Ah, okay."

She sighed. "I really do miss you, Daddy. Come home soon, okay?" Then she added, "And for the love of Mario Batali, will you go eat something decent?"

Gigi was still tackling her homework when the doorbell rang. She went to see who it was and had just made it to the top of the steps when her mom opened the door, revealing three fourths of the Stewart family: Finn, Ms. Marian, and Logan.

"Hi, Ms. Nancy," Finley said to Gigi's mom. "I tried to call earlier. I think I left my geography book in your car." She smiled up at Gigi and offered a little wave. Gigi halfheartedly waved back.

"Go take a look." Gigi's mom took her keys off the sunflower hook by the door and handed them over to Finn. "Don't forget to lock it."

"Sure," she said, darting over to the side door that led to the garage. "Thanks!"

"She told me as we were leaving ShopRite," Ms. Marian explained. "With a cart full of dairy and frozen vegetables. Sorry for the hit-and-run."

Gigi's mom waved her off. "Not a problem." Then she looked towards the upstairs landing. "Gee, what are you doing? Come down and say hi."

Gigi obliged just as Finn emerged from the garage, triumphantly holding her textbook. "Found it!"

"Great. Let's go, kiddos."

Even though things were still technically weird with Finn, Gigi piped up, "I'm working on geography too. Do you want to do our homework together?"

Finn looked surprised for a second. Then she nodded vigorously. Both girls flashed puppy-dog eyes at their mothers.

"I can bring her home later," Gigi's mom offered.

Ms. Marian nodded. "Be home by eight, okay?"

Finn started for the stairs before Gigi's mom headed her off. "Dining room," she said. "Gigi, go get your stuff."

Eff and Gee rolled their eyes at each other, but Gigi obliged.

They set up camp at the table.

"Hey, Gee?" Finn said.

"Yeah?"

"I feel really awful about what happened at practice."

"It's okay," Gigi said, wanting, very much, to mean it.

74

"No," Finley said. "It's really *not* okay. And I am really, really sorry."

Gigi could hear the sincerity in Finn's words. She smiled at her BFF. "Already forgotten," she said. "Besides, I know it was Fred's fault anyway."

"Fred?"

"Fred the Freckle," Gigi said. "He always was getting you into trouble."

Finley burst out into laughter. "I must not be feeding him enough."

"Well, let's get on it!"

They grabbed some snacks in the kitchen, then worked side by side on their assignment—drawing and labeling a map of ancient Greece. They finished it in about twenty minutes. This left them plenty of time before Finn needed to be at home.

"What do you want to do?" Finley asked.

"Party planning?"

"We're doing that Saturday," she said. "I need the extra time to percolate."

"Cupcakes?" Gigi offered.

"Yes!" Finn squealed. "You have to win that bake-off. What kind are you thinking?"

"I want to make one that tastes like a cannoli.

Doesn't that sound yum?"

"I'm drooling just thinking about it," Finn said. "Okay. Let's do this."

Gigi's idea was to adapt her mom's signature hot-milk cake recipe by swapping in ricotta cheese for the milk and adding some orange zest. She pulled the ingredients from their well-stocked fridge and pantry.

"Wet or dry?" she asked Finn.

"Dry."

So while Gigi was whisking eggs, ricotta, and vanilla, Finn was measuring out flour, sugar, and baking powder and sifting them into a big bowl. Gigi looked up at her friend, who sported the identical look of steely determination that she did whenever she was driving a ball down the soccer pitch. Her lips were puffed out and everything.

Next, Gigi added the wet ingredients into the dry ones. She stirred. Man, that batter was thick!

"Here, let me," Finn offered. As she stirred, Gigi could see, for once, a practical benefit to all of Finn's workouts. "What made you want to make a cannoli cupcake anyway?" Finn asked as she grunted through her task.

"My dad."

"He likes cannolis?"

"I don't know," Gigi said. "I guess I should ask him. He's in Italy—that's what made me think of it."

Finn stopped mixing. "Italy? I thought he was in Germany."

"That was two countries ago," Gigi said. "After Munich he went to Prague, and now he's in Milan."

"Oh."

After another minute of mixing, Finn threw up her hands. "I give up!" she said. "Can't we use the mixer?"

Gigi peered into the bowl. Serious thickness—like wet concrete. It was going to make for cake that was way too dense. "What if we add some liquid to loosen it up? Maybe a tablespoon of vinegar? Chef Angela says that a little acid can lighten a batter."

"On it."

Finn grabbed the bottle of white vinegar from under the sink, and Gigi went to retrieve the cupcake liners from the walk-in pantry. While she was trying to decide which ones to use, Finn cried out, "Gigi, come quick!"

She dropped the liners on the pantry floor and raced out just in time to see foaming batter streaming over the sides of the bowl. Finley was trying to squash the foam with paper towels, but it was growing too quickly.

"What happened?" Gigi said.

"I don't know!" Finn unwound more paper towels from the roll. "Make it stop! Make it stop!"

Just then, Gigi's mother materialized out of nowhere. "What in the—"

"Mama!" Gigi exclaimed. "Help!"

In a few swift movements, Gigi's mother scooped up the goopy bowl and deposited it into the sink.

"Smart," Eff and Gee said in unison. Then they looked at each other and started to laugh.

Gigi's mother took some fresh paper towels and patted some of the wayward goop from her shirt. "Girls, what did you *do*?"

"Must've been the vinegar," Finn explained.

"Vinegar?" Gigi's mother echoed.

"Yeah," Gigi said. "We added a tablespoon to lighten up the batter."

"No," Finn said. "We added a cup."

Gigi did a double take. "A cup?"

"I thought that's what you told me!"

"Either way," Gigi continued, "I don't understand why it went Vesuvius on us. I mean, vinegar only does that when it's combined with—"

"Baking soda," Finn finished for her. "There's baking soda in the recipe."

"No," Gigi said. "There's baking *powder*."

Finn shrugged. "You got baking soda from the pantry, so that's what I put in."

Gigi picked up the orange box on the countertop. Yep, baking soda. How could she have made such a rookie mistake?

The three of them stared at the bowl. It was *still* spewing a little foamy goop over the sides.

"Well then," Gigi said. "I declare this a certified batter disaster."

She and Finn broke out into peals of laughter. Gigi's mother, on the other hand, wasn't laughing.

"It's all fun and games until someone has to clean the kitchen," she said. "Guess what? It's not going to be me."

Despite her proclamation, Gigi's mother helped the girls mop up the remnants of the batter disaster. Three sets of hands made light of the work, and the kitchen was spotless in no time.

"I'm going to get changed," Gigi's mom said. "Then

I think we need to take Finn home—it's almost eight o'clock."

"I'm glad you came over," Gigi said as Finley gathered up her things.

"Me too," Finn said. "And even though it ended up a 'disaster,' it was fun baking with you. I'm going to miss it."

It took Gigi a few seconds to register what Finn was saying. "So you *are* dropping our cooking class. Like, definitely."

Finn nodded slowly. "Are you mad?"

"More like sad," Gigi said. "But I guess I kind of knew you'd pick the soccer thing."

And that you'd pick Lauren, the annoying little voice in her brain added.

"It's just that it's—"

"A really great opportunity," Gigi finished for her. "I know."

"Don't be mad," Finn pleaded.

"I'm not," Gigi assured her.

And she really wasn't mad, not like she had been at practice. No, Gigi really *was* sad. Even though she wouldn't dream of dropping the cooking class herself, and even though she'd had a great time getting to know Miranda, something about knowing that Finn would never come back with her to Chef Angela's again felt . . . *wrong*. Like she and Finn were taking another backwards step away from each other.

Gigi's mom reentered the kitchen. "You girls ready?"

Nope, Gigi thought. *I am not ready for any of this— not at all.*

CHAPTER 9

At school, Finn and Gigi had an unspoken agreement—pretend as if nothing weird was happening between them. They were so good at pretending that, within a day, Gigi had practically forgotten that anything *had* happened.

Until their next soccer practice.

Gigi trudged onto the field with grim determination. She wondered if Finn would get all up in her face again. She wasn't sure, but she did know this: if the tables had been reversed, and Coach had been giving Finn a hard time, Gigi would have stepped in to defend her BFF.

Gigi steeled herself for a showdown, but it never came. Finn was uncharacteristically passive at practice. There were no showy moves, no great displays of technical skill. No displays of anything, really. Finley kept her head down and her mouth shut.

And Gigi hated every minute of it.

As Coach divided the girls for scrimmage, Gigi pulled Finn aside. "What do you think you're doing?" she asked her.

Finn shrugged. "I don't know what you mean."

"Sure you do," Gigi said. "This? Isn't you."

"You don't like it when I'm me at practice," Finn said softly.

Gigi rolled her eyes. "That's not true. I just don't like it when you make fun of me at practice. I mean, you called me *Princess*."

"But . . . so what? I mean, you actually own more than one tiara!" Finn cried.

"That's different, and you know it."

Coach blew her whistle. "Stewart! Princess! Quit your gossiping—we've got work to do."

"Hey, Coach," Finn called out, her eyes still locked with Gigi's. "Can you maybe not call my best friend Princess? She, like, really hates it."

"If I promise not to call her Princess," Coach said, "will she promise to break a sweat?"

"Deal!" Gigi called over to her.

Now it was Coach's turn to roll her eyes. She blew her whistle again and yelled, "Come on, ladies, let's move those feet!"

Afterwards, as they headed back to the locker room to change, Gigi said, "See? Was that so hard?"

"It was excruciating," Finn joked. "Almost as bad as cleaning up the big batter disaster."

And just like that, Gigi felt the seesaw tip in the other direction. Like maybe—just maybe—Eff and Gee were back again.

It was Ms. Marian's turn to drive the girls home, and the atmosphere in her Jeep was completely different from the one in Gigi's mom's car just two days before. The girls chatted over each other, trying to cram two days of real conversation into the six-minute ride. It wasn't enough time, so Finn called Gigi the minute she hit the house, and they continued talking until Ms. Marian told Finley it was time for dinner.

"I gotta go," Finn said. "But . . . Gee?"

"Yeah?"

"I'm really glad we're not fighting anymore."

"Yeah," Gigi said. "Me too."

It was true. Gigi's heart felt a thousand pounds lighter. It wasn't like she and Finn had never disagreed before. They'd had their fair share of arguments. After nearly twelve years of best friendship, it would be hard not to.

But this had been the first time that Gigi had wondered if their best friendship was forever.

So many things were changing, and so quickly. Sometimes Gigi wished she could hit the pause button on her life.

Not forever—just long enough that she had time to catch up.

After school the next day, Gigi's mother took her to the craft store to pick up some tools she'd need for her first Purl Jam at the library. Gigi selected a fat pair of shiny pink knitting needles and a package of yarn (a skein, her mom called it) in dark teal. It was thin and supersoft and had little fluffy bits coming off it.

"You sure this is what you want?" her mom asked. "Because we could ask a salesperson for some advice. . . ."

"That's okay," Gigi said. "I'm happy with these."

That night, Gigi's mother dropped her off at the library. "I'm heading over to Yoga U," she told her. "It's hot yoga night!"

Why her mother voluntarily chose to sweat was beyond Gigi, but who was she to judge?

As she walked into the library, Gigi felt an unfamiliar shyness creep over her. She wasn't used to walking into strange situations alone. Her stomach fluttered as she walked up to the front desk, clutching a plastic bag with her new needles and yarn.

"Excuse me," she said to a college student checking returned books back in. "Can you please tell me where I can find Purl Jam?"

The girl pointed in the general direction of the library's music collection. "Try over there."

"Um, I'm looking for the knitting club?" Gigi explained. "It meets here on Thursday nights?"

"Oh, duh," the girl said. "I totally forgot they call themselves that. Trying to bring in a younger crowd, I guess." She put the stack of books she was working with down on the counter. "Follow me. I'll show you."

As she trailed behind College Girl, clutching her grocery bag tightly with both hands, Gigi's stomach flutters intensified. What exactly had she gotten herself into? Finn was probably sitting at home, just doing her homework or staring at her computer. Why hadn't Gigi invited her along?

Because not *inviting her is the whole point,* she reminded herself.

The Purl Jammers' meeting room was gray and bland. And speaking of gray, so were the knitters who formed the group. College Girl had said they were trying to entice younger members, and Gigi was younger *by far*. All but two members had silver hair. Of the other two, one looked to be about her mother's age (though unlike Gigi's mom, *this* woman sported several visible tattoos and two nose rings).

The last Purl Jammer wasn't a woman at all, but a man from Gigi's school: her tall, lanky math teacher, Mr. Baker. Just seeing him in the room made Gigi's cheeks flame hotly. In her head, Gigi tried to calculate the odds of escaping before Mr. Baker saw her, except that his eyes widened in recognition before she could even finish putting together the equation.

"Why, hello there, Gigi!" Mr. Baker said. "Come, come—let me introduce you." He waved her over.

Mr. Baker made a big deal out of making sure that everyone knew that Gigi was one of the top students in his class.

"Rock on," said Malissa, the nose-ringed woman, offering Gigi a fist bump. She liked Malissa, who kind of reminded her of Miranda—like a preview of the kind of adult Miranda might be. Without the pigtails, of course.

The group's leader, Mrs. Broderick, welcomed Gigi warmly as the others took their seats. "It's always so nice to see young people take an interest in knitting. What are you working on, dear?"

Gigi swallowed hard. "I'm not sure," she said. "I mean, I haven't actually started anything yet. I have yarn, though." She showed her and Mr. Baker the pretty teal stuff she'd gotten at the craft store.

"Oh," Mrs. Broderick said. "That's lovely. I have to say, I find eyelash yarn a bit tricky to work with. Have you used it before?"

Gigi shook her head no. "I've never actually knitted before. I was hoping that I would, you know, be able to learn. Here."

Mrs. Broderick and Mr. Baker exchanged a look that made Gigi's face turn even redder. A quick glance around the room told Gigi everything she needed to know: none of the Jammers was working on, say, a simple scarf. No, they were clickety-clacking their way through poufy berets, lacy shawls, and sweaters with complicated patterns.

"Let's have a look at your needles, shall we?" Mr. Baker said in his bright, cheerful way.

Gigi slowly pulled out the pretty pink pair she'd picked out earlier.

"Oh my," Mrs. Broderick said. "Those are . . ."

"Rather large," Mr. Baker finished for her.

"Especially for such a delicate yarn," Mrs. Broderick agreed.

Gigi sighed. First the batter disaster, and now this? Her judgment was proving to be anything but reliable lately.

"Pattern?" Mr. Baker asked.

Gigi blinked at him in response.

"Well, we can work with what we have," Mr. Baker said. "Now, let's wipe away that frown, Miss Prince. After all, there's no crying in knitting."

Except, there *was* a lot of crying in knitting—especially where Gigi was concerned. Crying on the inside, at least. For the life of her, she couldn't figure out why Julia Roberts claimed this was such a relaxing hobby. Casting the yarn on to the needle wasn't so bad. But beyond that? Everything had to be absolutely perfect. It wasn't like a stir-fry, where you could adjust the seasonings or add a new ingredient. In knitting, if you missed one wrong stitch, you could conceivably have to rip out entire rows just to fix it.

Gigi was grateful for Mr. Baker's patience. No matter how many errors she made, or questions she had, he never once got annoyed with her. Or if he did, he hid it very well.

"You're an awesome teacher, Mr. B," Gigi told him. "Thank you."

"That's very kind of you," he said. Then he leaned

in and stage-whispered, "Students like you make it all worthwhile."

Because of this, Gigi forced herself to smile through the pain. She felt like she owed Mr. Baker that much.

As she wrestled with the wretched eyelash yarn—which, by the way, was shedding all over the delicate beaded top she'd unfortunately chosen to wear—Mr. Baker explained to her how knitting incorporated mathematical concepts. He showed her the project that he was working on for his wife. It was one of those infinity scarves, only Mr. Baker called it a Möbius strip. He pulled out a picture of what the finished scarf would look like. "It looks like a continuous loop," he said, "but see that twist in the loop? That's what makes the Möbius strip so interesting. Despite its appearance, it's actually a one-sided surface!

"If you were to make a model out of paper, and tried to cut the strip down the center, you wouldn't end up with two Möbius strips," he continued. "No, you would end up with one much larger Möbius strip. You should try it! Or maybe we'll make one in class."

After ninety minutes, with Mr. Baker helping her every step of the way, Gigi somehow managed to get through four complete rows of something fairly narrow (a skinny scarf, maybe?). Because of the size of her needles and the slimness of the yarn, the result was something that had lots of loops and holes. In fact, it looked like several moths had used it for a buffet.

As the Jammers began to pack up their projects, Mr. Baker asked Gigi, "Will I see you back here next week?"

Gigi was nearly one hundred percent certain that she was not destined to become a true Purl Jammer, but Mr. Baker looked so eager for her to say yes that she couldn't bring herself to let him down. She settled on "Maybe."

"Thanks again for all your help, Mr. B. I'm really sorry I sucked up all of your time."

"Nonsense," he said. "It was my pleasure."

Gigi found her mother in the checkout line, clutching half a dozen books. "How did it go?" her mom asked.

Gigi shrugged. "It went."

"That bad?"

Gigi pulled out her holey project and held it up as evidence.

"It's . . . *unusual*," her mother said. "In fact, if you'd told me you'd crocheted it, I would say it looked rather advanced."

"I think we can both agree that I am not a Purl Jammer," Gigi sighed. "Knitting is way too stressful."

• • •

At home, in her room, Gigi shoved her knitting "project" and yarn deep into the bottom drawer of her desk. Then she took the yarn back out and looked at the angry lion poised like a regal king on the label. It made her chuckle. Such a fierce expression for such a frilly, delicate product!

With a small, pointy pair of scissors, Gigi carefully cut into the label and around the oval logo. This, she decided, needed to go on the Wall.

But as soon as she had that thought, it was replaced by another: *I can't put it there all by myself.*

In the nearly eight years that the massive collage had been in the making, Gigi had never actually pasted anything up on her own. The Wall was an Eff and Gee production, and every single item on it represented something that the two of them had done or thought or said *together*.

Even so, Gigi felt her massive knitting fail deserved to be memorialized in some way. And the Wall was in *her* room, not Finley's. She shouldn't feel guilty about wanting to add something to it. Should she?

She approached the wall, tape in hand. She raised the lion up and . . .

No, she thought, *the criteria for new Wall items that*

Finn and I have followed since birth just doesn't apply here.

She had no desire to proclaim a long life to knitting. Plus, where was she going to put the label? The Wall had been unofficially sectioned off into zones—birthdays, Halloween costumes, celebrities they were crushing on, LOL kitties . . . there wasn't a place designated for "Things I Will Likely Never Do Again."

Gigi lowered her hand. The logo would have to stay off the Wall . . . for now.

She tucked the cutout under her pencil cup for safekeeping, turned out the lights, and went to bed.

CHAPTER 10

As they boarded the bus after school on Friday, Gigi impulsively asked Finn if she wanted to come over. "I mean, I know we're hanging out tomorrow after your soccer thing," she said, "but I was thinking about trying out a new cupcake recipe. And since you can't come to class . . ."

"Yeah," Finn said. "I know. And dude, I'd love to, but . . ."

"But what?"

"Lauren asked me if I wanted to go to the mall. Her mom is driving us, but maybe you could meet us over there?"

Gigi didn't want to admit it, even to herself, but the fact that Finn had made plans with Lauren stung—*hard*. She knew she was being ridiculous. It wasn't as if Finn was *only* making plans with Lauren. And there had been plenty of times when Finn and Katie or Finn and Maggie had gone off and done something, just the two of them. Gigi didn't feel the teensiest bit jealous of them then. So why now? What was so different about Lauren Avila?

Everything is different about Lauren Avila! that awful voice in Gigi's head piped up. *Forget for a minute that she's in eighth grade and a star on the varsity soccer team. Lauren Avila is also effortlessly pretty. And everyone likes her!*

It was true. Lauren was tall, with long, lean legs and clear skin the color of honey. Her shiny hair dipped well past her shoulders and had the kind of bounce to it that Gigi thought existed only in shampoo commercials. She glowed without the help of any makeup, and her affection for argyle sweaters—which, by the way, looked fantastic on her—had spawned a copycat trend among the girls of Sterling Middle School earlier that year.

Becoming friends with pretty, popular Lauren Avila was going to change Finley, Gigi felt certain. Hadn't it changed her already?

Or maybe it was changing how Finn *saw* Gigi.

"Thanks for the invite," Gigi said, "but I'm not really feeling the mall."

Finn snorted. "Since when does Gigi Prince *ever*

turn down a trip to the mall?"

"I don't know," Gigi said. "Maybe I don't feel like crashing."

"It's not crashing if I invite you, dude. Just think about, okay? We're not leaving until six."

Gigi came home to an empty house and a note from her mother saying that she had had to cover for another volunteer at Dress for Success and probably wouldn't be home until seven o'clock. So Gigi couldn't have gotten a ride to the mall even if she did change her mind about going. Which she hadn't.

But if she did . . .

It might not be a bad idea to hang out with Finn and Lauren together. A trip to the mall would give Gigi a prime opportunity to get to know Lauren. It was not out of the question that she might like her as much as Finn did.

And hey, it couldn't hurt if Lauren saw how *close* Eff and Gee were—that Finley already had a best friend and didn't need any applications for a new one.

She called Finn and asked her if she could catch a ride with her and Lauren.

Finn hesitated, then said, "I don't know, Gee. It might be kind of weird."

"Weird? Weird how?"

"Well, Mrs. Avila doesn't know you, and you don't even really know Lauren yet, so . . ."

"Okay," Gigi said. "How about this? You tell Lauren to meet us at the mall, and we can get your mom to drive. Then Lauren's mom can just take us all home."

Gigi was pleased with herself for coming up with such a perfect solution. Finn, however, was not as impressed.

"It's just that . . . if we do it your way, then it pretty much changes the plans I made with Lauren," Finn said carefully. "Plus, my mom wasn't thinking she had to drive anywhere tonight, and my dad's working a double, so she'd have to take Logan with us too."

Gigi let out an exasperated sigh. "What if I just walk over to your house? Or do you think that would be weird too?"

"Dude," Finley said. "You sound like you're mad at me or something."

"I'm not," Gigi replied . . . though if she were honest, she *was* a little annoyed by Finn's resistance. "Look, you're the one who said I should think about coming. If I can't get a ride with you, I can't come."

"Hold on," Finn said. She must've muted the phone, because Gigi didn't hear anything for the next minute or so. When she clicked back on, she said, "Okay. Mom said you can come here. Only she said you have to call your mom first, to get permission, and then you have to make sure you're at my place by four thirty, because she doesn't want you walking over in the dark."

Gigi wasn't sure why Ms. Marian didn't just come get her, but she didn't say that to Finn. Instead she said, "Okay. See you in a bit."

Next, she tried calling her mom, but her cell phone went straight to voice mail. So did the line at Dress for Success. Frustrated, Gigi headed up to her room to pick out an outfit for the evening.

It had grown progressively cooler over the week, but the mall was notoriously overheated during the fall and winter. Layers were likely Gigi's best bet. She rummaged around in her dresser until she located a lime-green-and-navy argyle sweater vest she hadn't worn in a while. It was a teensy bit short, but she figured she could layer it up with a longer button-down underneath and go for a retro vibe. Navy leggings and a cropped jean jacket would complete the look.

Gigi tried her mother again but kept getting voice mail. A quick look at the clock revealed that she only had about fifteen minutes before she had to leave for Finn's. How could she get her mother's permission if her mother refused to answer a phone?

The minutes ticked away. Gigi spritzed her curls with a little water to help them plump back up, then changed into her mall outfit. She grabbed twenty dollars from the hamburger-shaped bank in her room, tucked the bills into her wristlet, pulled on her Sperrys, and headed back downstairs.

It was four ten; in five minutes, she was going to have to leave. She made one more attempt to reach her mom, and when she got her voice mail for the twelfth time, she decided to leave a message: "Hey, it's me, I just wanted to let you know that I'm going to the mall with Finn. Love you! Bye."

When she got to Finn's house, Ms. Marian answered the door. "Hey, cutie," she said. "Come on in. Just watch your step."

Gigi's eyes widened as she took in the front hall. Nearly every inch of the floor was covered with stuff: stacks of books, piles upon piles of clothes, mountains of sports equipment, and tons of Logan's old toys. No wonder Ms. Marian couldn't come get her. Their house was a mess, and it looked like Ms. Marian was working hard to tame it.

"Don't mind all this," Ms. Marian said. "Just getting ready for tomorrow's wee-cycle sale."

"Tomorrow's *what*?"

"Wee-cycle sale," Ms. Marian repeated. "It's like a flea market for moms, with all kinds of gently used kid stuff."

"Oh," Gigi said. "That's, uh, cool. Is Finn in her room?"

"Go right on up."

The door to Finn's bedroom was closed, so Gigi knocked. No answer. Gigi knocked again. Still no answer. Gigi tried one more time.

"WHAT?" Finn hollered, flinging the door open. "Oh, it's you. Sorry. Logan hasn't stopped bothering me all afternoon. Um, what are you *wearing*?"

Gigi smoothed the front of her sweater vest and asked, "What do you mean?"

"Nothing," Finn said. "Never mind."

Gigi could feel her face heat up. "I'm making a fashion statement?"

"You're making something. Hey, let's go grab some snackage."

The floor of the kitchen was almost as full as that of the entryway. Gigi nearly tripped into a tub of action figures but steadied herself against the fridge. "So," she said, when she'd found her footing, "you think my outfit looks bad?"

"I didn't say that."

"Your face kind of did."

Finn shrugged. "You look fine," she said. "You just don't look like *you*. That's all."

Gigi's immediate instinct was to shoot back, "Well, you aren't acting like you, so I guess this makes us even." But instead she held her tongue.

"Salty, sweet, or chewy?" Finn asked.

"How about all three?"

"Gorp it is!" Finn said, grinning. She pulled down a large mixing bowl, and the girls started filling it with little bits of everything: good ol' raisins and peanuts, of course, but also M&Ms, mini marshmallows, pretzel nuggets, Goldfish crackers, and a generous shake of Cap'n Crunch. The crazy snack mix was a holdover from their days as Girl Scouts, and a tradition they maintained long after they hung up their Brownie vests.

Finn grabbed the bowl, and the girls headed into the den.

"So what's at the mall?" Gigi asked.

"Stores," Finn replied. "A fast-food court. Aggressive salespeople trying to convince you that their Dead Sea skin-care products will get rid of your acne."

Gigi cocked her head to one side. "I know that, silly. What's the *reason* we're going?"

"You've never needed a reason before."

"*I* don't," Gigi said. "But *you* hate going to the mall without a specific mission in mind."

Now it was Finn's face that was starting to redden. "I don't have a mission. I just . . . Lauren asked me to go, and I said yes."

"She's probably on the prowl for more argyle," Gigi muttered without thinking about it.

"A-ha!" Finn said, pointing at Gigi. "I knew that's why you wore that vest. I don't get it, Gee. You act like you hate Lauren, but clearly you want her to like you. Why is that?"

"Because *you* like her!" Gigi cried. "She's your friend, and you're my best friend, and I guess if I want to keep spending time with my best friend, I need to find a way to be friends with her other. Best. Friend."

"OH MY GOD," Finn said. "She is not my best friend. She is just a *new friend*. Dude, why does that make you so crazy? Am I not supposed to be friends with anybody *but* you?"

"No," Gigi said. "Obviously, no."

"Well, then stop acting like that's the case! It's starting to get really annoying."

Annoying. The word hung out there like a big ugly cloud over both of their heads. Gigi didn't know how to respond, and if Finn's sudden silence was any indication, she didn't either.

Finn flicked on the television and flipped through the channels until she came upon a SpongeBob episode. Gigi had long loved the cartoon, but Finn wasn't as big a fan. When she left the TV on the show, Gigi figured it was a peace offering of sorts.

They sat and watched, not saying another word. The bowl of gorp sat between them and remained untouched.

Lauren Avila's mother looked nothing like her daughter. She was short, for one thing, and what her Mom-Mom referred to as "pleasingly plump." Her hair was quite a few shades darker than Lauren's, with strands of silver spider webbing through it, and she smelled like cinnamon.

Add to that her tinkly laugh, and Gigi couldn't help but love her.

If only she could say the same about her offspring.

To be honest, it wasn't even Lauren's fault. She was nice enough to Gigi—polite, asked her questions, and even complimented the now-contentious sweater vest. Finn, on the other hand, did her absolute best to make Gigi feel one hundred percent excluded. Everything she said to Lauren sounded like a foreign language to

Gigi; every conversation was one long in-joke. After a while, Gigi tuned out entirely.

Because it was Friday night, the mall's teen curfew hours were in effect, which meant that the girls weren't allowed to be there without parental supervision. This was fine when they stopped for dinner at Noodles & Company, but once in the mall itself, their little foursome divided into two pairs: Lauren and Finn walking ahead, with Gigi and Mrs. Avila bringing up the rear.

"Do you play soccer as well?" Mrs. Avila asked Gigi.

She nodded. "But I'm not nearly as good as those two."

Mrs. Avila cocked her head to one side. "Is it a competition?"

"Aren't all sports?" Gigi said. "Like, by definition?"

"Maybe," Mrs. Avila said. "Though I believe it's far better to compete with yourself than to compare yourself to someone else. After all, no one can do a better job of being you than you."

Gigi thought Mrs. Avila sounded a lot like Yoda, only without the weird sentence structure.

This night was not turning out as Gigi had hoped. She'd wanted to demonstrate to Lauren the rock-solid bond that Eff and Gee shared. Instead, Finn's antics ended up proving the exact opposite.

She'd have been completely miserable without Mrs. Avila, who kept up a steady stream of pleasant conversation as they walked. Between her and the Purl Jammers, Gigi was starting to wonder why it was that only old people seemed to enjoy her company these days.

The minutes ticked by, slow and painful. Gigi regretted her decision to go to the mall. She could've been at home, eating leftovers and trying out new cupcake recipes before tomorrow's cooking class. She could've been figuring out what to tackle next on her list of potential hobbies to pursue. She could've been sitting in the dark, doing nothing and saying nothing, and still probably would have been happier than she was watching Lauren and Finley become BFFs right before her eyes.

Just after eight, Mrs. Avila's cell phone rang. She answered it smiling, but her face grew concerned almost immediately. Then she handed the phone to Gigi.

"It's your mother," she said. "She wants to talk to you."

Gigi's breath caught in her throat. *Daddy*, she thought.

"Mama?" she said. "Is everything okay?"

"No, it most certainly is *not*. Gillian Gemma

Prince, how dare you! Leaving this house without my permission, with people I have never even met? You get your butt home right this minute, you hear me? Now give the phone back to Mrs. Avila. Please."

Ice water filled Gigi's veins, and she shivered as she passed the phone back over.

Finn and Lauren turned and stared at Gigi as Mrs. Avila spoke to her mother a few feet away. "What happened?" Finn asked.

"I think I need to go home," Gigi said. "I'm really sorry."

Mrs. Avila rejoined the group. "Ladies, I'm feeling rather tired. Okay if we head out?"

The girls all nodded.

"Good," Mrs. Avila said. "Gigi, I'm going to drop you off at your place. You can tell me the way?"

When they pulled up in front of the Princes' house, Mrs. Avila put the car in park and said, "Gigi, let me walk you to your door. I'd like to say hello to your mother."

As the two made their way up the walk, Mrs. Avila said to her, "Try to breathe, honey. It's going to be okay, I promise."

Gigi's mother didn't seem to be screaming angry when she answered the door. A little stern, yes. Concerned, definitely. But angry? Not so much.

Mrs. Avila introduced herself and said some things that Gigi couldn't focus on. There were apologies exchanged, and at one point, Mrs. Avila said, "I really enjoyed meeting your daughter. She's a lovely girl, and you raised her to have impeccable manners." This made her mother smile, even if it was only for a second.

When they were alone, Gigi's mother let loose. "Explain to me why, after Ms. Marian told you that you must have my permission before going over to her house, you decided that obtaining said permission wasn't necessary?"

"I couldn't get ahold of you," Gigi explained. "I left you messages, and a note."

"Back up," her mom said. "You couldn't get ahold of me, therefore you couldn't get my permission—therefore you *should not have left the house*. Yes?"

"I guess so, but—"

"No buts!" Gigi's mother said. "You should not have left the house. Say it."

"I should not have left the house," Gigi repeated.

Her mother sighed. "You're almost twelve, Gigi. I thought you were mature enough that I could leave you alone for a few hours without you getting into trouble."

"But I didn't get into trouble!" Gigi protested. "I

walked to Finn's house while it was light out. You let me do that all the time. And then I went to the mall with a grown-up that Ms. Marian trusts."

"But *I* hadn't met her," her mother said. "*I* hadn't said yes. That's my point. Why was it so important for you to go in the first place?"

Gigi considered telling her mother all about Lauren Avila, but she already felt like a big enough loser. So instead she said, "I'm sorry, Mama. I shouldn't have gone."

"Thank you," she replied. "Lesson learned?"

"Lesson learned," Gigi agreed. "Am I grounded?"

Gigi's mother considered the question. Then she said, her voice softer, "No. Not this time. Next time, I will not be so kind, got me?"

Gigi nodded vigorously. "Thank you," she said. "Although . . ."

"What?"

"If you wanted to, you know, ground me from soccer for a couple of weeks, I wouldn't blame you."

Her mom laughed. "Gee, if you hate soccer so much, why do you play?"

Good question, Gigi thought. But she didn't answer. Instead, she gave her mother a quick hug and a kiss on

108

the cheek. "I love you, Mama," she said. "And I really am sorry."

Then she headed up to her room, snuggled in with Glamour Puss, and called it a night.

CHAPTER 11

Gigi walked into the Open Kitchen with a plan in her pocket and a fire under her bum. She marched straight towards Miranda, who was sitting alone, staring off into space. Gigi plopped her stuff down next to her and said, "I have two words for you: tiramisu cupcakes."

"Tirami-*what*?" Miranda said.

"Tiramisu. Come on, you've never had tiramisu? It's, like, the standard dessert in any decent Italian restaurant. Besides cannoli, but I already tried that and it didn't work out so well for me. Anyway, are you in?"

Miranda's black eyebrows knitted together. "Slow your roll, Gigi Prince. I have no idea what you're talking about."

Gigi sucked in a deep breath, blew it out fast, and started over. "Remember how last week you said that we should enter the cupcake bake-off as a team?"

"Yes," Miranda said coolly. "And I also remember

you saying you already had a partner."

"Well, I don't," Gigi said. "Finley isn't coming back to class. So I thought—"

"Your BFF bailed on you, so *now* you want me to be your partner?" Miranda interrupted.

"Not exactly," Gigi said. "I mean, okay, yes, I thought that this was something Finn and I would do together, and that isn't happening. But it's not like you're a pity choice. I had so much fun with you last week. And I think you're right—if we work together, we'll be unbeatable."

"Well, duh," Miranda said. "We'd totally rock it. But I don't know. To be honest, it didn't feel so great when you shut me down."

"It didn't feel so great to me, either," Gigi admitted. "I thought about it a lot. I would've called you, but I didn't have your number."

Miranda opened her metal lunchbox purse and pulled out an iPhone wrapped in a pink rubber bunny case, complete with ears and tail. "Let's fix that. Swap digits?" She typed some things and thrust the phone at Gigi.

"This is totally embarrassing," Gigi said, "but I don't have my own phone. I'm trying to get my mom to buy me one for my twelfth birthday."

"So give me your home number. And your email addy—I'll send you my info."

While they were completing this transaction, Chef Angela called out, "Listen up, kiddos! Today we're going to be making the perfect triple-chocolate cupcake: dark chocolate cake, milk chocolate filling, semisweet chocolate icing. It's so good, it'll make your mama cry. Let's get started!"

Gigi heard a few grumbles—two of her classmates didn't like anything chocolate, while another declared the entire recipe "lame." But not Miranda, who professed that mastering basics made her the happiest "because that way you can make anything."

"I like the way you think," Gigi said.

The girls worked side by side, following Chef Angela's recipe and instructions. They learned that adding sour cream to a cake helps emulsify the batter, making the cake tighter and moister, and that replacing a bit of the liquid with coffee makes it taste that much more chocolaty. They learned how to make a velvety ganache in the microwave without burning it. They learned how to cut a little cone-shaped chunk out of the top of a cupcake so that you could add filling, then trim the pointy bit off the bottom so that you could plug it back up.

The ninety-minute class flew by. Both Gigi and Miranda kept working on their cupcakes, even as their fellow classmates began to pack up their things.

"Nice work, ladies!" Chef Angela declared after reviewing their final products.

"Have one," Miranda offered. "I added a little something special to the batter."

Chef Angela took a bite and chewed it thoughtfully. Then she took another, and another. Finally her eyes flew open in surprise. "Cinnamon!" she said. "Girl, that is genius. I might have to try that myself."

The girls made sure to clean their stations, especially because Gigi had, as usual, made a little bit more of a mess than everyone else. As she wiped the last chocolate smudge off the counter, she turned to Miranda and said, "You should come over sometime soon. We can have a sleepover and practice recipes all night."

"Cool, like tonight?"

This gave Gigi pause. Technically, she still had plans with Finn. But after last night, she wasn't so sure. And besides, Finley had blown her off so many times lately, who was to say she wouldn't do the same thing again? Why should Gigi give up spending time with a new friend for the mere *possibility* of Finn actually showing up? Too bad she had no way of getting in touch with her to see if they were still on or not.

Gigi made a mental note: another perfect example of why she needed a cell phone for her birthday.

"Let's do it," she said to Miranda.

"You sure?"

"Yes," she said firmly. "You think your parents will say yes?"

"It's just me and my mom," Miranda said. "But it should probably be okay. Let's go ask her."

Miranda pointed to a tall blond woman with sleek hair pulled into a low ponytail. She was dressed in various shades of beige and looked like someone from an L.L. Bean catalog. In other words, she looked nothing like Miranda.

"*That's* your mother?" Gigi asked.

Miranda rolled her eyes. "Yeah, I know. I'm not adopted, if that's what you're thinking. I mean, I used to think I was, because we are so totally different, but it turns out I just look an awful lot like my dad."

They walked over to Miranda's mom, who Miranda introduced as Regan.

"Nice to meet you, Ms. Regan," Gigi said.

"Oh, just call me Regan," she responded. "Please. I prefer it."

Gigi wasn't sure what to say to this—she was fairly certain her mother would flip if she called someone else's mom by their first name alone. So she just smiled.

Miranda filled (Ms.) Regan in on her and Gigi's plans for the evening. "It's cool if I do that, right?"

Regan's pale eyebrows furrowed together. "What does Gigi's mother say?"

The trio headed outside to find Gigi's mom, who liked to listen to audiobooks when she drove alone, and who tended to wait in the car when picking up Gigi, so she could squeeze in another chapter or two.

Gigi knocked on the window, which her mother promptly rolled down. "This is my friend Miranda," she said.

"Hiya," Miranda said with a wave.

"And this is Miranda's mom, Regan," Gigi continued, adding quickly, "She asked me to call her that—just Regan—and anyway, can Miranda spend the night tonight?"

"But I thought—"

"Yeah, that's not happening," Gigi said, cutting her off. "I want *Miranda* to spend the night. Her mom said it's okay if you say it's okay."

"Those were not my exact words," Regan corrected. "I was headed over to Brew HaHa to get some coffee. I don't know what your schedule is like, but maybe you could follow me over there? We could chat for a few minutes, get to know each other a little better."

"Sure," Gigi's mother said.

On the car ride to the coffee shop, her mom asked, "Did Finn cancel on you again?"

"Sort of," Gigi said. "I don't really want to talk about it."

Her mother sighed. "Okay."

"And please don't go running to Ms. Marian about any of this," Gigi asked.

"What do you mean?"

"Come on," Gigi said. "Do you have any idea how hard it is when your mom is best friends with your best friend's mom? It's like having four people in a best friendship!"

Gigi's mom let out a deep, loud laugh. "You, my dear, crack me up."

At Brew HaHa, Gigi and Miranda got creamy cups of hot chocolate and ginormous chocolate chip muffins. ("These are bigger than a baby's head!" Miranda declared.) They sat a table away from their mothers and plotted their evening, confident that their sleepover request would be granted. Miranda pulled a little Hello Kitty notebook and a fat pen from her lunchbox purse and opened to a fresh page. First up was working on their entry for the bake-off, of course. But which recipe to try?

"I vote tiramisu," Gigi said. She explained to Miranda how she'd pulled a bunch of recipes and was planning on combining them.

"Right on!" Miranda said. "You rock."

"Yeah. Unless I'm trying to make a cannoli cupcake, that is." Gigi filled Miranda in on her most recent kitchen disaster. But instead of laughing, as some girls might, Miranda simply shook her head in sympathy.

"We've all been there," she said. "We have all been there."

In the end it was decided that Miranda's mom would drop her off at Gigi's around three; Miranda would come armed with a bucket of mani-pedi supplies; Gigi would start pulling all of the ingredients together for her Frankensteined tiramisu cupcake recipe; and her mom would order Grotto's pizza for dinner.

In other words, it was shaping up to be a most excellent Saturday night.

On the ride home, Gigi said, "Thanks for doing this, Mama."

"You are more than welcome," her mother said. "But Gigi—"

Here it comes, Gigi thought. *Lecture time.*

"Don't let this thing with Finley fester for too long," her mom said. "Girlfriends fight. That's normal. Not talking about *why* you're fighting, or not working together to find a way to resolve it—that's how friendships *end*."

An involuntary chill ran through Gigi's entire body. She didn't like to think about not being friends with Finn. In fact, she couldn't really imagine it at all.

CHAPTER 12

Gigi was straightening up her room in preparation for Miranda's arrival when the phone rang. It was Finn's landline, and Gigi froze. Had she guessed wrong about Finley?

The ringing stopped. A few seconds later, Gigi heard her mother call up the stairs, "Gigi, phone!"

"Hello?"

"Hey," Finn said. "It's me."

"Hi."

"So here's the thing," Finn said. "I know I'm supposed to come over this afternoon, but—"

"But you can't," Gigi finished for her. "Because of something that has to do with Lauren."

Her words were met with pure silence, so much so that Gigi wondered if their call had gotten disconnected. "Hello?" she said into the receiver. "You still there?"

"Yeah," Finn said. "And it's not that I *can't* come

over. It's just that . . . well, Lauren's dad scored some last-minute tickets to the Union match, and she asked me if I wanted to go."

"The what now?"

"The Union match," Finn said. "It's the pro soccer team in Philly."

"Oh, right."

"And you know how I've been dying to go see a real game—"

"Actually," Gigi said, "I didn't know that."

"Well, I have been," Finn said. "I really, really have. And the best part is that Lauren has an extra ticket for you too. Isn't that awesome?"

"Awesome" was not the first word Gigi thought of when it came to going to a professional soccer match, but she didn't say this. Instead, she said, "I can't go. I have a friend coming over."

"Who?" Finn asked.

"Miranda."

"Weird Girl? From cooking class?"

"She's not weird," Gigi said. "She's my friend."

"Oh," Finn said. She paused a moment. "That's cool."

Gigi thought she might have heard a note of sadness in Finley's voice. But then Finn said, "So you're okay if I go to the game then?"

"Yeah, sure," Gigi said, resigned.

"You're the best, Gee," Finn said. "Call you tomorrow, 'kay?"

But Gigi had a feeling that Finn wouldn't call tomorrow. In fact, she was pretty sure that at some point soon, Finn wouldn't be calling her at all.

One of the first things Gigi learned about a Miranda sleepover was that girlfriend came prepared. In addition to a literal bucket of mani-pedi supplies—a rainbow of polishes, glitter, decals, sparkling jewels you glued on in fun patterns—she brought:

A Hello Kitty sleeping bag, complete with a pillow shaped like Hello Kitty's head

A fat stack of cooking magazines

Two decks of cards

Several half-used pots of finger paints

An electric-blue camera

But the best thing Miranda brought was her big plastic box of cake-decorating supplies. It was the fancy purple-and-white one they sold at craft stores—the one that had compartments for just about everything you could think of, including specially marked slots for all the different decorating tips. Better yet, Miranda had almost every single decorating tip in it!

"Jealous!" Gigi declared, looking through the collection. "Where did you get all of this?"

"Ebay," Miranda said matter-of-factly. "That's about two years' worth of birthday, Christmas, and Easter money right there."

"You bought it yourself?"

Miranda nodded. "I even sold some of my old books and video games at 2nd and Charles to raise the cash."

Gigi was impressed. She'd never known anyone so enterprising. There was that time that Kendall had "saved" up for the American Girl Girl of the Year doll, but since her grandparents had given her the majority of the cost, she wasn't sure that counted.

They ate dinner in the family room, wearing their pajamas even though it was only five thirty. In fact, Miranda arrived wearing hers, a pair of pink polka-dotted pants matched with a long-sleeved T-shirt. She held a pair of blue Cookie Monster slippers in one hand and said apologetically, "My mom told me I had to wear real shoes on the way here."

As they munched on pizza, the girls watched old episodes of *Good Eats* on the Cooking Channel.

"Don't you just love Alton Brown?" Miranda said in a dreamy, breathy voice. She sounded like Katie did when she talked about her latest Hollywood crush object.

"He's pretty cool," Gigi agreed.

"You know, he was my first cooking teacher," Miranda said.

"Like . . . in person?"

"Well, no," Miranda said. "But, like, his show? That's where I first learned the difference between the creaming method and the muffin method, and how important it is to measure dry ingredients by weight instead of volume."

"You weigh your flour?"

Miranda's eyes widened. "Don't you?"

Gigi laughed. "I guess I will tonight."

After dinner, the girls rolled up their sleeves and got down to the very serious business of cupcake baking. Gigi showed Miranda the recipe she'd patched together, as well as the inspiration recipes. Miranda sized them up like a scientist. With a pencil, she did some quick math calculations on a piece of scratch paper, then made a couple of adjustments to Gigi's recipe. Gigi stared at her in amazement.

"It's all about ratios," Miranda explained. "If you reduce the flour by two ounces, it will weigh slightly less than the sugar, which will make the cake a little more tender. And if we add an extra egg yolk, we'll get a smoother cake that's moist but holds its shape."

"Unbelievable," Gigi said, shaking her head. "You're like some kind of genius."

"Nah, just some kind of math nerd."

But Miranda was being modest. She really *was* a genius. Or, at the very least, she was someone who took her baking super seriously. Gigi watched her work, fascinated. First, Miranda checked the oven thermometer to make sure the heat inside matched what it was supposed to be. ("Five degrees off—not bad!") Then, halfway through baking the cakes, she rotated the pans so that they would cook evenly. "I don't know your oven," she said. "So frankly, I can't trust it. Yet." Miranda made sure to chill the metal mixer bowl in the freezer for fifteen minutes before starting the mascarpone cream topping. "It keeps the fat matrix from collapsing," Miranda explained, and even though Gigi had no idea what she meant, she nodded her head like she did.

"Where did you learn all of this stuff?" Gigi asked, beyond impressed.

"I told you," Miranda said, smiling. "Alton Brown."

They assembled the cupcakes together, but instead of just dusting cocoa powder over the top, Miranda pulled a block of semisweet chocolate from the pantry and, using a vegetable peeler, made little shaved curls to garnish.

Gigi reached for a cupcake, eager to try the new concoction, but Miranda gently slapped her hand away.

"These need to set overnight," she said.

"You're really going to wait until morning?"

"Sure," Miranda said. "What could be better than cupcakes for breakfast?"

"True."

After the girls had cleaned the kitchen top to bottom—a feat that impressed Gigi's mother in a major way—they headed up to Gigi's room to work on their nails. But Miranda took barely two steps into the room before stopping short and exclaiming, "What *is* that thing?"

It took Gigi a few beats to realize that Miranda was referring to the Wall. "Oh," she said. "That. I guess it looks a little crazy if you're not used to it."

Miranda walked up to the Wall and ran her finger along some of the images. Gigi watched her drinking them all in. Seeing the Wall through Miranda's amazed eyes made Gigi feel even sadder.

"So you and Blondie really have been best friends forever, huh?" Miranda said.

"Yeah, I guess."

"You're lucky," she said. "I've never had a BFF like that. Ever."

This gave Gigi pause. She'd never known someone who was completely best friendless. Sure, plenty of the girls at her school had spent time in between best friends, but that was normal.

"Why not?" Gigi asked. "I mean, just curious."

Miranda shrugged. "My mom and I moved around a lot when I was younger. In fact, Fletcher's the first school I've ever attended for more than a year." She laughed, then added, "Also, I'm not sure if you noticed, but some people find me a little weird."

"But you're a good weird," Gigi reminded her.

Miranda *was* rather quirky. The perpetual pigtails, the superfunky clothes, the blunt way she spoke to people . . . these things had put Gigi off to begin with. But their shared appreciation for the culinary arts helped Gigi see past all of that surface stuff, and want to get to know the girl underneath.

And, she was finding, she was very very glad that she did.

"Knitting, French club, clarinet, fencing . . . wow, you have one serious to-do list," Miranda said.

Gigi's head snapped over to her desk, where

Miranda was reading off the items she'd written in her composition book. She fought the urge to run over and snatch it away from her.

"It's not a today to-do list," Gigi said. "It's just some stuff I want to do eventually."

"Like fencing?"

Gigi's face flushed hotly. "Yes, like fencing. I read somewhere that it was one of Angelina Jolie's hobbies when she was a kid. And Kiera Knightley looked kind of cool swinging her sword in *Pirates of the Caribbean*."

"Oh, it *is* cool," Miranda said without a hint of sarcasm. "Like, crazy cool. And not something I would ever expect your BFF to be into."

"She's not," Gigi said. "I mean, she might be, if I asked her. But I didn't. I mean, it's not like I do *everything* with Finn."

Miranda waved her hand along the length of the Wall. "Either way, this is some serious history here. So, um, what's the story behind number eight?" She gestured towards Gigi's notebook.

Number eight? Gigi peered over at the open page. Oh, right.

Find a new best friend?

"It's nothing," she said quickly. "Just me being dumb."

Miranda's right eyebrow arched upwards.

Gigi squirmed a little. Discussing the Finn situation felt uncomfortable, like she was going behind Finley's back or something.

"Anyway," Gigi said, "part of the reason I made that list was because I wanted to do more stuff on my own. I'm actually going to this free fencing class tomorrow. You should totally come!"

Miranda burst out laughing. "Um, doesn't bringing a friend kind of defeat the whole purpose of doing more stuff on your own?"

Gigi frowned. "I guess so."

"It's way nice of you to ask, though," Miranda said. "Why don't you call me tomorrow afternoon and tell me how it went?"

"Deal."

Miranda turned away from the Wall and pulled a vinyl tablecloth from her backpack. She shook it out and placed it in the middle of the floor. When Gigi shot her a quizzical look, Miranda said, "Duh, to catch the drips."

"Drips?"

"From the nail polish," she explained, dumping all her nail supplies out on the tablecloth, then sorting them based on function and color.

They started with their toes. Miranda painted hers neon green, while Gigi opted for a hot pink. Then they switched polishes, and Miranda dipped a straight pin nestled in a pencil's eraser into Gigi's Passion Pink to put polka dots all over her big toenail. "Want me to dot you up?" she asked Gigi.

"Yes, please!"

When their nails had gotten dry to the touch, Miranda carefully extracted her camera from the front pocket of her backpack. "We simply must document this momentous occasion," she said, in a really bad British accent. "Hold up your hands."

Gigi obliged, Miranda snapped the picture, and what looked like a piece of white paper shot out from the bottom of her camera.

"What was that?" Gigi asked.

"It's the picture," Miranda informed her. "It's a Polaroid camera. Instant film."

The only cameras Gigi had ever seen or used had all been digital. In fact, most of the time her mom didn't even bring her camera, opting instead to use the one built into her phone.

"That," Gigi said, "is crazy cool. Can I see it?"

Miranda handed her the camera, and Gigi asked if she could take a picture.

"Sure," Miranda said.

Gigi trained the camera on Miranda, then paused. "Better idea," she said. "Let's take one together."

The girls huddled together, their heads smushed together in classic selfie formation. Gigi snapped a picture of the two of them grinning. Even before it developed, Miranda said, "Take another one, so we can each have a copy."

Gigi stared at the rectangle of white as their faces begin to appear on it. "Amazing," she said. "Like magic."

When the photo dried, she thought about how badly she wanted to paste it onto the Wall. But, as was the case with the lion label from the yarn, something about that impulse didn't feel quite right.

Then it hit her—she'd start a new Wall! There was a clean stretch from the left-hand corner on down. Gigi scrambled over to her desk drawer and pulled out some paint-safe foam tape, then snagged the lion label from under her pen cup. Then, on the new Wall, which was perpendicular to the first one, Gigi pasted the label and, overlapping it slightly, tacked on the totally adorable Polaroid of her and Miranda.

"There," Gigi said, feeling satisfied. "I will call it 'Wall Two-Point-Oh.'"

"Nice," Miranda said. "And hey—thanks for thinking I'm Wall-worthy."

It was such a small thing, really. Starting the new Wall. But in that moment, it felt like some giant gesture to Gigi. And if the perma-grin on Miranda's face was any indication, it felt good to her too.

CHAPTER 13

When Gigi woke up the next morning, she peered over the side of her loft bed. Miranda was sprawled out on top of her sleeping bag, reading through an issue of *Food Network Magazine* with a flashlight. She shined the light up on Gigi's face. "You're awake."

"Yeah," Gigi said through a yawn. "Have you been up long?"

"Um, sort of," she said. "I mean, do you even know what time it is?"

Gigi looked over at the alarm clock that sat at her desk. The big digital numbers read 8:32. "It's not that late," she said. "I thought your mom wasn't picking you up until ten."

"She's not," Miranda said. "But let me ask you again: do you know what time it is?"

"Yes, it's eight thirty-two."

"Who cares about clock time?" Miranda said. "It's *cupcake time!*"

"Ohmigod," Gigi said. "Tasty goodness!"

"Race you downstairs!"

Miranda got there first and immediately pulled the airtight container of cupcakes from the fridge. "They're even prettier than I remembered."

Gigi reached for one. She peeled the wrapper down some and went in for a bite.

"Wait!" Miranda exclaimed. "Don't eat it yet!"

She ran out of the room, and Gigi could hear her feet pounding up the stairs, and then back down. Miranda reappeared with her blue Polaroid camera.

"Okay," she said. "Dig in."

As Gigi's teeth sank through the creamy pile of mascarpone topping and into the velvety cake, Miranda snapped a pic. Then she handed the camera over to Gigi and said, "My turn!"

The two girls ate their entire cupcakes, chewing thoughtfully.

"It's good," Miranda said finally.

"But not great," Gigi chimed in.

"Yeah, and I'm not sure why. It's got the right amount of sweet, but . . ." Her voice trailed off. "But it's missing

133

something. Or is it just because I've never had tiramisu before?"

"No, you're right," Gigi said. "This won't win us the bake-off."

Of course, that didn't stop them from eating another cupcake once Gigi's mother joined them in the kitchen. "It would be rude to let your mom eat alone," Miranda said. "Right?"

Later, as Miranda packed up to head home, Gigi asked her again if she wanted to go to the fencing class with her.

"Nah," Miranda said. "It's nice of you to ask, but this is a you thing, not an us thing."

Gigi remembered how hard it had been to walk into the library to meet up with the Purl Jammers and felt a little jolt of panic strike her insides.

"You'll be fine," Miranda said, almost as if she could read Gigi's mind. "Just pretend you're Angelina Jolie."

Miranda's words ran through Gigi's head as she entered the Chinese American Community Center. Her mother was right behind her, as Gigi insisted she at least walk her in. In the gym, where the class was held, a handful of kids Gigi's age, and some younger, milled around a table displaying what Gigi assumed was fencing equipment—lots of long swordlike things and mesh masks like you see people wear in the movies. On one side, parents sat in metal folding chairs. There was a knitter in the bunch, working on something wide that pooled in her lap in a big, shapeless lump. There were a few moms and dads glued to their iPads, and one woman absorbed in a paperback book.

Gigi turned to her mother. "You have to stay."

"No, the gentleman I spoke with said that wasn't required."

"Mama!" Gigi whisper yelled. "Look around! *Everybody's* parents are staying."

Her mother surveyed the room. "Fine," she said. "I'll stay. But for the record, I think you're perfectly capable of being here by yourself. I raised you to be a strong, independent—"

"Yeah, okay, fine," Gigi said, cutting her off. "Now go sit down. Over there. With the other parents. Please."

Gigi sized up the kids looking at the equipment. From what she could tell, there were four boys and one other girl. The boys looked like they were in fourth or fifth grade, Gigi thought, but the girl looked way younger. She was really short—Gigi guessed her head

135

wouldn't even reach Gigi's shoulders—and stick thin, with long black hair that ran down her back like water.

She took a deep breath and said to herself, "I am Angelina Jolie. I am smart, I am fierce, and I don't care what anybody thinks of me."

Except that last part wasn't true. Of course she cared what people thought. It didn't help that her mother had waited until the last minute to tell her she needed to wear sweatpants to the class. The only pair she could find in her drawers was lavender and had a bedazzled patch on the front right thigh that read GURLZ RULE! in swirly, sparkly letters.

The pants were from last year, and just a little on the short side. Gigi kneeled down as if to tie her sneaker, but instead yanked the cuffs into the proper position. Oops. Nope. Now her waistband was well below her belly button. If she stood and lifted her arms even an inch, she'd be baring midriff—a definite no-no in the Prince house. She sighed, pulling the pants back up. Her sock-covered ankles were exposed. How was she supposed to feel confident like *that*?

More kids filtered in, and a bunch of them seemed to know each other already. The girl, however, stayed off to the side by herself. Gigi wondered if she felt awkward too. Remembering how fearless Miranda had been when she introduced herself, Gigi decided to walk up and say hello.

"I'm Gigi," she said to the girl, extending her hand just like Miranda had. "What's your name?"

The girl smiled but left Gigi's hand dangling there. "I can't shake," she explained. "Mother forbids it. Too many germs. I can bump your elbow, though." She pointed her elbow at Gigi and thrust it towards her.

"Uh, okay." Gigi mirrored the girl's action, and they tapped elbows lightly. The girl nodded at her, then turned away. "Wait! I still don't know your name," Gigi called after her. Too late. She was already on the other side of the gym.

Gigi wondered if Mother had forbidden the girl to reveal her name to strangers too.

Finally a tall, gray-haired man walked to the center of the gym floor and clapped his hands. "Kids, gather round. It's time to get started. Please, have a seat," he said, gesturing to the floor.

They dutifully sat in a semicircle, arcing around the man, who introduced himself as Winston Abrams the Third. ("But you may call me Mr. Win," he told them, flashing a toothpaste commercial smile.)

"Today," he said, "I am going to introduce you to the art of fencing. How many of you are already familiar with this art?"

A few hands shot up, including that of the nameless elbow bumper.

"Excellent," Mr. Win said, rubbing his palms together. He looked a little like Mr. Burns from *The Simpsons*, and this thought made Gigi giggle.

Mr. Win began by showing them the various "weapons" used in fencing and told them that today they'd be learning how to use the basic foil. Next, he held up a lamé, which was a weird metallic vest that, when touched by the foil, registered points during the match. This was due to some cord that plugged into the vest and connected each fencer to the scoring machine. Mr. Win began suiting up in front of them, walking them through the various pieces of equipment and explaining what each one did.

"Today you'll be using the club's equipment," he explained. "If you decide to take lessons, you may continue to borrow equipment for the first session. After that, you must begin to purchase your own. Now, let's get you outfitted for the lesson."

Mr. Win snapped his fingers, and two assistants magically appeared. Each student was given a lamé, a mask, and a glove, and explanations on how to put them all on. At first Gigi was thrilled—these were so much cooler than the stinky pinafores she had to wear for soccer—but after a couple of minutes she realized just how hot the fencing equipment was. She had a feeling that once she started moving around, heavy sweating was sure to follow.

Why on earth had she chosen this again? Oh, right. Angelina Jolie. Keira Knightley.

"The first thing you must learn in the art of fencing," Mr. Win said, "is how to stand *en garde*."

Mr. Win spread his legs shoulder-width apart and squatted down some, pushing his right arm—the one holding the foil—out from his side and curling his left into a chicken wing, hand resting on hip.

"When you are *en garde*," Mr. Win said, "you must be certain that your knees are directly over your toes." He bounced a few times to demonstrate, and it looked so silly to Gigi that she had to fight the urge to giggle again.

"Now," he said, "we advance."

Advancing looked a lot like crab walking, only your body was turned in the direction you were moving. Retreating, the next thing he showed them, was pretty much advancing in reverse. "It's imperative that you move heel first, not toe. Heel first!"

Next, Mr. Win demonstrated the lunge, which looked very similar to the kinds of lunges Gigi had done in soccer practices. Only in a fencing lunge, the hand holding the foil was extended, as the fencer's goal was to touch the tip to the lamé to score points. Next, he demonstrated the parry, which was how fencers blocked the lunge attack. This involved moving your foil so as to block your opponent's. "The key to a successful parry," he said, "is small movements. Let me repeat: *small* movements."

Gigi looked around. All of the kids were staring at Mr. Win, seemingly mesmerized. None of them looked like they were trying to stifle laughter. But all of a sudden, to Gigi, the whole fencing thing seemed extremely *ridiculous*. What was *wrong* with her? She turned to catch her mother's eye, but her mom was chatting up one of the iPad moms and didn't even notice.

Mr. Win began to pair up students so that they could practice on each other. Since Gigi and the girl with the elbows were the only two girls, Mr. Win decided to put them together.

Gigi faced her much-shorter opponent and offered her a smile before pulling the mask down over her face. Elbows was so tiny, Gigi would have to take it easy on her.

"*En garde!*" Mr. Win shouted, and everyone assumed the position. Then Mr. Win walked around, critiquing each of them. Of Gigi he said, "Too loose. Tighten up here and here," and tapped each knee with the tip of his foil. "Also here and here," he added, tapping both of Gigi's shoulders. The nameless germophobe's stance, however, was proclaimed "Excellent," and she was given no further coaching.

Next, Mr. Win directed everyone on Gigi's side of the line to practice advancing on his call. "*En garde, ready, fence!*" he boomed. Gigi crab walked towards the girl in front of her, foil extended, but before she even had a chance to think about aiming for the girl's torso, Elbows flashed her foil against Gigi's so swiftly that Gigi dropped the thing altogether.

Gigi's jaw dropped under her mask. "I take it you've done this before?" she said to the girl.

"No," the girl replied. "I'm just naturally good at everything I do."

Gigi blinked at her.

The girl lifted her mask and smiled at Gigi. "That was a joke. Sort of. This isn't my first time fencing. I learned at camp with Mr. Win last summer."

"A ringer," Gigi said, more to herself than the girl. "I see how it is."

She kept at it, though. After a few more pathetic lunging attempts, Mr. Win declared that it was time to switch sides. Gigi hoped she'd be better at parrying than she was at lunging, but Mr. Win had barely finished his "*En garde*, ready, fence" call before her opponent had expertly stabbed her lamé. This went on three more times, and on the last touch—a lunge made with a guttural battle cry—Gigi realized the girl had tackled all four quadrants of the vest.

Okay. So she had tried fencing.

Gigi stepped backwards, stripped the mask from her sweaty face, and held her hands up in defeat. "Stick a foil in me," she said. "I am *done*."

CHAPTER 14

On the ride home, Gigi's mother said, "So you're not a fencer. It's okay. You don't have to like everything you try. That's why you try things to begin with."

"I'm not a fencer, I'm not a knitter," Gigi muttered. "Maybe this whole list thing was a dumb idea. Maybe I should just stick with the things I already know I'm bad at, like playing soccer."

Her mother said, "Gillian Gemma Prince, for the hundredth time, if you hate soccer so much, why don't you just quit the team?"

She didn't want to give her mother the real answer, which was that soccer was one of her connections to Finn. If she quit, wouldn't it be another nail in the coffin of their friendship?

"Quitting soccer is not an option," she told her mother.

"But why?" her mom pressed.

"Because everyone at school has to play at least one sport," she reminded her. "If it wasn't soccer, it would be softball or field hockey or"—she shuddered—"*track*."

"Point taken."

As soon as she hit the house, Gigi headed for the shower. She was so sweaty and gross from the fencing class, and the hot water felt like a hug.

She was pulling a wide-toothed comb through her long red curls when her mom knocked on the bathroom door. "You almost done in there? Daddy's on Skype, and he wants to talk to you."

"Be right out!"

Gigi tightened the belt on her fuzzy blue bathrobe and threw open the door. "Which computer?" she asked breathlessly.

"Kitchen."

Gigi flew down the stairs, skipping steps as she ran. "Daddy!" she cried as soon as she saw his smiling face. "It's so good to see you. I miss you!"

"I miss you too," he said. "Now what's this I hear about you putting up a fence?"

"Not a fence, Daddy," she laughed. "Fencing class. As in, I took one. And guess what? I am really, really, *really* awful at it."

"You? I don't believe it."

"It's true," she said. "I'm hopeless. But it's okay. I still haven't tried horseback riding or clarinet or writing for the school newspaper. Maybe I'll be better at one of those things. But even if I'm not, the whole point of the list was for me to try new things on my own, which is what I've been doing. So that's good, I guess."

"Pause, Gigi," her dad said. "Rewind. Start with this list of which you speak."

Gigi took a breath, then gave her dad the highlights (if you could call them that) of everything that had been happening the past two weeks.

"And the worst part," she finished, "is that Finn and I *still* haven't started planning our birthday party. You know, besides the fact that our almost twelve-year best friendship might be ending."

Her dad said, "I guess what I don't understand is why you need Finn to plan the party. If I remember correctly, you're the one who usually dreams up the big ideas to begin with."

"Well, yes," Gigi admitted. "But I never make any real decisions without Finn. And the last time we even talked about the party, I wanted a Broadway theme and she was going in a completely different direction. Dad, she wanted us to go indoor rock climbing."

He let out a big, deep belly laugh, the kind that

made Gigi grin reflexively. She wished she could reach through the laptop screen and give him a monkey hug.

"Here's an idea," he said. "Instead of doing what Finn wants, or trying to convince her to want what *you* want, why not just plan a party that you know will make the two of you happy? Start it on your own, as your birthday present to Finn. If she decides she wants to help out, welcome her back. Either way, I know you'll end up with a rockin' party."

"Don't say 'rockin','" she said. "But otherwise, you are a genius, Daddy. When are you coming home again?"

"Within the next week," he said. "Hopefully in time for your first soccer game."

"That's good," she said. "I know you wouldn't want to miss me warming the bench. If you're lucky, you can see me standing on the field doing nothing!"

He rolled his eyes at her playfully. "Look, Gee, we all know you're destined to be a star. But you don't have to be a star at everything. It's good to let the others shine from time to time."

"Did Mom tell you to say that?"

"Nope," he said. "I just know my little girl."

"Don't say 'little girl.' I'm almost twelve."

He responded with a smile that bordered on sad. "Don't I know it."

Gigi thought about her father's suggestion all afternoon. What was stopping her from taking matters into her own highly capable hands and planning a totally awesome party that both she and Finn would love? Best case scenario, she and Finn would make up and they'd have their usual double birthday blowout. Worst case scenario—the one in which Finn did indeed ditch her for good—she'd still get to celebrate her birthday in style.

They were already so behind schedule. Emily Post etiquette dictated that invitations should be sent four weeks in advance, and since the party would likely be on April 11—the Saturday between their birthdays—they had missed that mark yesterday. If Gigi had any hopes of pulling this thing off in time, she'd have to hustle. The invites would simply have to go out within the week.

Gigi grabbed her composition book and turned to a new page. At the top she wrote *Potential Birthday Party Themes*. Underneath, she wrote *Bright Lights of Broadway*. Then, remembering what her dad had said about not trying to convince Finn to want what she, Gigi, wanted, she crossed it out. No, she'd have to do better than that.

She thought of the gorp she and Finn had mixed up Friday night. That was something they still had in common. But a Girl Scout–themed birthday party wouldn't exactly fly with their friends, and it was still a little too cold for camping. Plus, Gigi wasn't much of a camper. A *glam*per, maybe, but definitely not a sleep-in-a-tent-outdoors kind of camper.

Gigi chewed on her pen cap. The only thing Finn seemed really nuts about lately was soccer. She supposed she could plan a soccer-themed party. That would definitely make Finn happy. But it would also make Gigi pretty miserable.

There had to be a compromise, but if she didn't think of something soon, they might very well end up with a purple-themed party after all.

She decided to switch gears. She turned the page and wrote *To Do Today* at the top. Then she started listing all of the tasks crowding her brain: coming up with a suitable party theme, finding a new recipe for the cupcake bake-off. . . .

Miranda! Gigi remembered that she'd promised to call after the fencing class. She logged on to her email account to retrieve Miranda's number.

"So, how did it go?" Miranda demanded, without so much as a hello. Gigi told her all about Mr. Win and the nameless elbow bumper and how she was one hundred percent, rock-solid certain that fencing wasn't in her future.

Miranda said, "I'm really glad you called—"

"Me too!" Gigi said. "I'm so glad we became friends. Aren't you?"

"Um, yeah, of course," Miranda said. "But I was actually talking about something I dug up today. See, I realized that all of the cupcake recipes you'd been trying out for the contest were inspired by Italian desserts. Which made me wonder what *other* Italian desserts were out there that could be translated into cupcake recipes.

"Anyway, I did some research, and it turns out that this Thursday is St. Joseph's Day. It's this Italian holiday honoring Jesus's stepdad. One of the main traditions is a pastry called a *zeppole*."

"I've had them!" Gigi exclaimed. "They're like doughnuts."

"Some are fried like that," Miranda said. "Others are baked, more like cream puff shells. Either way, I was thinking we could do a simple vanilla cupcake and then try out a bunch of different fillings. We can pipe cream on the top and then, just before serving, top that with a miniature zeppole. What do you think?"

"It sounds tasty," Gigi said. "When should we start?"

"We can email each other all week to work out the recipe. And then maybe we can try it out next Saturday?"

"Or what about Friday?" Gigi asked. "If you come over after school, we can work on the cupcake that night and take it to class on Saturday. That way we can get Chef Angela's opinion. She's not a judge, so it wouldn't be like we were cheating or anything."

"Excellent idea," Miranda said. "It's a plan."

After they hung up, Gigi checked her school planner to see if she had any outstanding homework assignments. There were two math worksheets she needed to finish for Mr. Baker's class, half a chapter in her social studies text left to be read, and—how could she have forgotten?—a French vocab quiz she had to study for.

French quiz . . . wait a minute, she still hadn't investigated French Club! She made a mental note to ask Madame Fournier about it after class tomorrow.

• • •

A couple of days later, on Tuesday, Gigi headed to French Club with a cooler bag full of chocolate mousse. What luck that her first French Club meeting happened to be on the very day they were having a food party!

When she'd talked to Madame Fournier about joining, her teacher seemed surprised. "It's so late in the year," she said. "We don't often get new students in the spring. But of course you are welcome. In fact, we're having a celebration on Tuesday."

Gigi wasn't quite sure what French Club would be like; when she'd asked, Madame Fournier said, "What happens in French Club stays in French Club." She offered up a knowing smile and tapped the side of her nose lightly with her pointer finger.

Gigi thought, *Okayyyy*. But she told Madame Fournier she'd definitely be there.

The door to Madame Fournier's room was closed, and Gigi took a long, deep breath before opening it. She half expected to see the room swathed in a French flag, with an Eiffel Tower statue planted in the center of the floor. Instead, Gigi was startled to see that everything was green. Green plastic tablecloths with four-leaf clover patterns covered blocks of desks, and a cardboard cutout of a leprechaun winked at her from

Madame Fournier's desk. It was far more Emerald City than City of Lights.

The French Club was having . . . a St. Patrick's Day party? Did the French even celebrate St. Patrick's Day?

"*Bonjour*, Gigi," Madame Fournier greeted her. "*Ça va?*"

"Oh, I'm fine, thank you. How are you doing?"

The head of every student in the classroom whipped around, and seven pairs of eyes lasered in on Gigi.

"*Non*," said Vanessa, a seventh grader Gigi had known since they were in elementary school together. "*Réessayez.*"

"*En français*," Madame Fournier added.

"Oh, okay," Gigi said. "I mean, *d'accord*. Um, *je suis très bien, merci*." She felt pleased with herself and smiled at her new French Club friends. "I brought some chocolate mousse. I made it myself. Well, my mom helped. Anyhoo, where should I pu—"

Vanessa shook her head. "*En français. Se souvenir?*"

"Uh . . . *oui?*" Gigi said. "I would like—um, *je . . . voudrais . . . un souvenir.*"

"*Souvenir* is a verb," Vanessa explained. "Not a noun. It means 'remember.'"

"Oh," Gigi said. "*Je suis* . . . sorry?"

"*Désolée*," Vanessa whispered.

Gigi flashed her a grateful smile. "*Oui. Je suis désolée.*"

Madame turned towards Gigi and said, "*Nous parlons toujours français dans le club de français.*" Gigi turned the words over in her head. She knew that *dans* meant "in" and was pretty sure that *toujours* meant "always." As for *parlons* . . .

"*Oui,*" Madame Fournier said. She smiled warmly at Gigi. "*C'est difficile au début, mais vous allez vous y habituer.*"

Gigi stared at her blankly. Then she looked at her new friend Vanessa, who shrugged as if to say, "I don't know what that means either."

"*C'est difficile,*" Madame repeated slowly, gesturing to the club's members.

"It's difficult," several said in unison.

She nodded. "*Au début.*" When no one responded, she held up one finger and said again, "*Au début.*"

"At first?" a skinny blond boy piped up.

"*Oui. Excellent!*" Madame Fournier smiled broadly at the boy. "*Mais . . .*"

"But . . . ," the club translated.

"*Vous allez vous y habituer.*"

More blank stares.

She said it again: "*Vous allez vous y habituer.*"

Still no takers. Madame Fournier drew in a deep breath. "*Vous . . .*"

"You . . . ," they said back.

"*Vous allez vous y habituer.*"

Pin-drop silence.

"It's difficult at first, but you'll get used to it!" Madame Fournier said, sounding rather exasperated. She sighed. Then, in a softer voice, she said to Gigi, "You will. Get used to it, I mean. *Nous parlons en français* because it makes it easier for you to learn."

Gigi nodded, but what she was really thinking was, *Um, I still haven't figured out how to conjugate* aller.

Gigi sat through the rest of the meeting. The conversation swirled around as she got by with a well-placed *oui* or *non*. As she picked at her perfect mousse, she thought, *Finn would laugh so hard at this.* And then, *She'd probably make up some crazy French-sounding words so the two of us could pretend we were participating.*

Gigi sighed. All this effort was supposed to distract her from being apart from her best friend. But sitting here, Finn was still pretty much all she could think about.

• • •

After the French Club fiasco, Gigi decided the best course of action was to focus on the cupcake bake-off. At least for now.

She thought about the zeppole cupcakes that Miranda wanted them to tackle. Gigi Googled "St. Joseph's Day" so that she could learn more about it. This led her to search for "Italian holidays," which led to a search on "Italian travel." She landed on a page outlining "100+ Things You Need to Know if You're Going to Italy." There, under the section titled Culture, Gigi saw the thing she didn't even know she was looking for until she'd found it.

"Sunday is a holy day—and not just for church, but for soccer!"

An enormous lightbulb went on over Gigi's head. *Italy*. It was perfect. Fantastic food, fun fashion, and fierce football (which is what the Europeans apparently called soccer). It was the best of Eff and Gee, all wrapped up in one gorgeous, theme-party-friendly package!

Plus, her dad was still in Milan, at least for a few more days. Gigi was sure if she asked him to pick up some authentic Italian things for the party, he'd totally do it. She wondered if it would be warm enough to hold the shindig outside.

Gigi's head swirled with thoughts of fountains and

gondolas and the Leaning Tower of Pisa. Would it be better to have a pasta bar or a build-your-own-grilled-pizza bar? She wondered if her parents would let her create a minifestival in their backyard. They could set up a bocce ball court, a gelato cart, and—oh! There could be a runway show, like it was fashion week.

And instead of a birthday cake, they could have an assortment of all of the cupcake recipes she'd been trying out. Gigi had a feeling that Miranda could help her fix that cannoli one, easy peasy lemon squeezy. She wondered if Miranda would mind helping her cater the whole event.

Would that be weird, though? Having Miranda at the party? She wouldn't know anyone, but Miranda was Gigi's friend now, so it only made sense to invite her.

Then it occurred to Gigi: the same held true for Lauren Avila. With a sinking feeling, Gigi began to resign herself to the fact that, now that Lauren and Finn were officially friends, she'd have to be included on all future guest lists too.

Wait. Why was she upset? Gigi decided right then and there that her jealousy of Lauren—because, she could admit to herself, that's really what it was: *jealousy*—had to go. There was no room—no *time*—in her life for such ugly feelings. She had a party to plan! And a cupcake bake-off to win! And a *To Do Someday* list that was sorely in need of a win.

What had Miranda said? "Jealousy is a wasted emotion."

She was totally right about that.

Gigi turned back to the someday to-do list, closed her eyes, and dropped her finger down randomly. When she looked, she saw that she was pointing to item number three: *Play clarinet*. Hmm. She would have to ask her mother if she could drive her into school early the next day, so that she could speak to the band teacher, Ms. Panettiere, about joining the woodwind section.

After all, learning an instrument couldn't be any more disastrous than what she'd already experienced, right?

CHAPTER 15

Gigi had never actually spoken to Ms. Panettiere; she knew her mostly from assemblies and the holiday concert. She was one of the younger teachers at Sterling Middle School, pretty and fashionable to boot, and the older girls liked to gossip about which of the boys had crushes on her.

In the past, walking into a strange teacher's classroom would've turned Gigi into an electric ball of nerves. But lately, all she ever seemed to be doing was walking into places she'd never been and talking to people she'd never met.

No big deal. I got this, she thought.

Ms. Panettiere was bent over her desk, scribbling furiously in a notebook. Gigi knocked on the open door to get her attention.

"Hello there," Ms. Panettiere said warmly. "How may I help you?"

"I'm interested in joining the band," Gigi said.

"Oh!" she said, the surprise registering in her voice. "Okay. Well, what instrument do you play?"

"I don't," Gigi said. "Yet. I want to learn the clarinet. I think."

Ms. Panettiere nodded. "It's a lovely choice. Do you have a sibling who played?"

"No. I'm an only child."

She smiled. "Let's back up a little. I'm Ms. Panettiere, but everyone calls me Ms. P. And you are . . ."

"Gillian Gemma Prince. But everyone calls *me* Gigi."

"So, Gigi, what made you interested in the clarinet?"

"Julia Roberts."

Ms. P's head tilted to the side. "I don't quite follow."

"She's this actress—"

"I know who Julia Roberts is," Ms. P said, another kind smile spreading across her face. "But I'm not quite sure what she has to do with the clarinet."

"Oh," Gigi said. "She played it. In high school. She was in the band."

"And you admire her?"

Gigi nodded. "I feel this—what does my mom call it?—*kinship* with her, 'cause she's got curly red hair like me."

"Ahh," Ms. P said. "I see. What grade are you in, Gigi?"

"Sixth."

"Good," Ms. P said. "So here's the thing: it's pretty late in the school year to join the band, let alone take up a brand-new instrument. But you know, in a couple of months you'll be selecting your classes for next year, and maybe over the summer you could take some private lessons to get you caught up."

Wait, what was Ms. P saying? Was she telling Gigi that she *couldn't* join the band?

Even though Ms. P was being super nice, and even though everything she said made complete sense, Gigi still felt like someone had sucker punched her in the gut.

Sure, there were still three other items on her someday to-do list (four, if you counted number eight), but in that moment, "play clarinet" was everything. Not because of Julia Roberts, or even because she'd had some lifelong burning desire to be a musician (she hadn't). It was just that right then and there, Gigi couldn't imagine failing at *yet another thing*, especially without even having the chance to try it first.

"Is everything okay, Gigi?" Ms. P asked. "You look a little upset."

"Sure," Gigi said. "I just really, really, really wanted to play the clarinet. I don't know if I'd even like it, or be good at it or whatever. But I really, really, really wanted to try."

Ms. P looked at her thoughtfully, her eyes squinty and lips scrunched in a way that said "My brain is working overtime." Then she asked, "What are you doing after school today?"

"I have soccer practice."

"And tomorrow?"

Gigi shook her head. "Nothing."

Ms. P lightly slapped her hands on the edge of her desk and said, "It's settled then. You come to the band room tomorrow after school, and I will give you a private clarinet lesson. And if you decide that this is something you want to pursue, I'll talk to your parents about renting you an instrument and getting some lessons. Sound good?"

"Good? That sounds *great*," Gigi said, her heart filling up like a balloon of gratitude. "Thanks, Ms. Panettiere. I mean it . . . thank *you*."

She was rewarded with a thousand-watt smile. "It is my sincere pleasure, Gillian Gemma Prince," she replied. "I like your fire. Must be the hair."

Gigi grinned. "Something like that."

• • •

Her victory in the band room put Gigi in an absolutely fantastic mood. She was so chipper, in fact, that nothing could seem to bring her down: not the pop quiz in geography, not the run she discovered in her brand-new purple tights, and not that Mrs. Dempsey *still* refused to reveal what the spring musical would be, even though auditions were scheduled for a week from Monday.

Then came lunch.

Typically, Gigi brought her lunch from home. Despite the fact that the Sterling Middle School cafeteria had supposedly improved its options this year, Gigi had a feeling that was only in the nutritional sense. Taste-wise, the menu left an awful lot to be desired.

But this morning, in her great rush to get to school early enough to see Ms. P before homeroom, Gigi had blown by the fridge and completely forgotten to grab the insulated sack she packed meticulously each night. If she'd had a cell phone, she could've texted her mother to ask if she wouldn't mind bringing it to her (just another reason why she *had* to have one for her birthday). Instead, the only thing Gigi could do was whip out the emergency school lunch card her mom had loaded with twenty dollars at the beginning of the school year. So far, Gigi had used the card exactly once.

The menu board outside the cafeteria listed KLUX DELUX CHIX PATTY SANDWICH and WACKY VEGGIE MAC as the main dish options. That didn't sound so bad. Gigi wished it all maybe *smelled* a little better, but beggars couldn't be choosers.

Gigi was trying to figure out what made the veggie mac so wacky when she felt an insistent tap on her shoulder. She turned to see Kendall, a look of grim determination on her face.

"Hey," Gigi said. "What's up?"

"I could ask you the same thing," Kendall said. Her hands were balled up on her hips. "What is going on with you and Finley?"

"What do you mean?" Gigi asked. Had Finn said something to their group? The idea was too awful to contemplate.

"You guys never went anywhere without each other," Kendall clarified. "Now it's like you're never together, and Finn's always hanging out with Lauren Avila!"

"Oh. That."

"Yes, *that*," Kendall said. "Are you going to stop being friends with her?"

"What? Why? What did Finn say?"

Kendall sighed. "She told Katie that you were mad at her, and when Katie asked why, Finn said it was because she was, like, really good at soccer and you're not."

Gigi was fairly certain that Finn would never say such a mean thing, but the words hurt nonetheless.

"She also said that Finn said that you're jealous because she's friends with an eighth grader," Kendall continued. "And then this morning, Maggie asked Finn about your guys' birthday party, and Mags said that Finn said that the two of you couldn't even have a conversation about it without you getting really weird about the whole thing."

"Weird?" Gigi echoed. "I might be weird. You know, if we actually *had* a conversation about it. Every time I try to plan stuff, she totally bails on me to go hang out with Lauren."

"So you *are* jealous!" Kendall exclaimed. "I get that. Remember when Katie broke her arm in third grade and everyone made this huge deal about it and started fighting over who got to write more stuff on her cast? And the thing that I wrote—like, *first,* before everyone else—got totally crowded in so that you could barely even see it? I was *totally* jealous."

Gigi shook her head in disbelief. "This is nothing like that, I assure you."

"Then what's your deal?" Kendall asked.

Gigi didn't know how to respond. Sure, *she* knew things between her and Finn weren't okay, and clearly *Finley* was aware that something was off as well. But Gigi had thought that the two of them were doing a pretty good job of keeping everyone *else* out of that particular loop. They sat together at lunch, carpooled home after soccer practice, and even had a brief phone conversation on Sunday night, though their six-minute chat consisted mostly of a) Finn gushing about the Union soccer match she and Lauren had attended the previous evening and b) double-checking the assignment due in English the next day.

"I've just been really busy," Gigi said after a pause. "And so has Finn. But we're fine, Kendall. I swear."

Kendall eyed her suspiciously. "Are you sure?"

No, not really, she thought. But she said, "Absolutely," in what she hoped was a convincing way.

"That's good," Kendall said. "I mean, you're *Eff and Gee*. There's, like, no you without her, and no her without you."

Gigi shook her head as if to clear the debris of this awkward, uncomfortable conversation. But not before she thought, *Maybe that's the problem.*

She picked up two grayish-green lunch trays and

handed one off to Kendall. When she reached the server, she asked for the Klux Delux.

"Gross," Kendall whisper screamed. To the server, she announced, "I'll have the Wacky Mac, please!" A thick, yellowish blob dotted with clumps of green landed on the foam plate with a sickening plop.

Gigi vowed right then and there that she would never, ever forget her lunch again.

All afternoon, Gigi kept replaying her conversation with Kendall. She knew her friend had a tendency to exaggerate, but she also knew that Finn must've said *something* to set her off. Rather than let this niggling feeling fester, Gigi decided it would be better to simply ask Finn straight up.

In the locker room before soccer practice, Gigi steeled herself and said, "Can we talk?"

"Uh, sure," Finley said. "What's up?"

Gigi paused, unsure how to say what it was she needed to say without stirring up any more drama.

"Kendall . . . ," she said, her voice trailing off.

Wait—was it her imagination, or did Finn just tense up when she said Kendall's name?

"What about her?" Finn asked stiffly.

"Somehow she got the impression that I am jealous of your mad soccer skills."

"Um . . . ," Finn said. She was staring at her cleats, tightening her laces, tugging at them extrahard. "I didn't say you were *jealous*. I just said there was some . . . tension."

"Because you're good at soccer and I'm not?" Gigi asked, incredulous. She couldn't believe she even had to ask the question in the first place.

Finn's silence felt like a solid response to Gigi.

"That," she said to Finn in a soft, quiet voice, "really hurts my feelings."

"Why?"

"Because I would never be *this* angry with you for something as dumb as that! And I am really, really, *really angry*!" As she spoke the words, Gigi felt the full weight of them. She'd had no illusions about her ability on the soccer field. The *only* reason she even stayed in soccer—besides the school's rule about playing for a sports team—was because of Finley. To support *her*. To spend time with *her*. Because that's what friends *did*.

"I'm sorry, Gee," Finley said. "I was frustrated. If I knew venting to Katie would've gotten back to you, I never would've done it in the first place."

167

Gigi shook her head. "That's not the point."

"Then what is?"

"You should've told *me* that you were frustrated," Gigi said. "Not Katie. Or if you did tell her, you should've told me afterwards. We don't talk behind each other's backs. At least, we never used to."

Before Finn could respond, Gigi shot up from the locker room bench and stormed out onto the field.

Quitting soccer would leave her with few options; the only spring sports offered for girls at Sterling Middle were softball, track, and co-ed lacrosse—none of which appealed to Gigi. Next year was a different story. Next year, she could go out for cheerleading in the fall, or even join the marching band's color guard. Backflips and dance-filled flag routines were much more her speed than kicking a stupid ball across a stupid soggy field.

For now, she'd just have to suck it up, keep her head down, and grit her teeth through what would be her very last soccer season ever.

Last one ever. Somehow, this thought cheered Gigi up. As Coach sent the team off to do their traditional warm-up laps, Gigi trotted along at a decent clip.

"Looking good, *Prince*," Coach called out as she ran by.

Gigi smiled and waved and kept on running.

Soon she was aware that Finley was running next to her. "You were right," she said to Gigi. "I should've talked to you directly."

Gigi looked at her, turned away, and ran faster.

Of course it didn't take much for Finley to match her pace. Finn said, "So . . . what? You're not going to talk to me now?"

Gigi drew in a big, deep breath and ran even harder. Her lungs burned and her legs ached, but she pressed on.

Finn fell in step almost immediately. "I can keep this up all day," she said. "You might as well accept my apology."

There was no way Gigi could pull ahead now; she was maxed out. So Gigi did the only thing she could do in this situation: she stopped cold.

Taking a sharp left, Gigi headed back to the locker room. Coach yelled, "Get back on the track, Prince. You've got two laps to go."

"I don't feel well," Gigi called over her shoulder as she marched past. "Taking a sick day."

"HALT!" Coach barked. She jogged over to Gigi and said, "If you leave now, you can't play in Sunday's game. Team rules."

Gigi knew right then and there that leaving was the only way to insure that Finn wouldn't follow. There was no way *she* would miss Sunday's game.

Gigi swallowed hard. "I . . . I'm good with that."

Coach's eyes narrowed, like she was sizing Gigi up. "You sure about this?"

She wasn't, but she nodded anyway, her chin quivering slightly.

"Okay, then," Coach said, with a firm nod. "I'll see you Monday." After changing back into her school clothes, Gigi headed to the principal's office. Mrs. Meara, Principal Weir's ancient assistant, was clicking away at her computer. Gigi cleared her throat, but Mrs. Meara didn't look up.

"Um, excuse me," Gigi said finally. "May I please use the phone to call my mom?"

Mrs. Meara didn't answer.

"Excuse me," Gigi repeated loudly. "May I please use—"

"What's that?" Mrs. Meara barked at her, her eyes never leaving the computer screen. "You're mumbling."

Gigi was pretty sure she wasn't, but she cleared her throat and tried again. "MAY I PLEASE USE THE—"

"Sure, you can use the phone," Mrs. Meara said. "You don't have to yell about it."

Gigi promptly burst into tears.

"Oh, doll, what's the matter?" Mrs. Meara asked, her demeanor instantly softening. "Here, let me get you a Kleenex."

She handed Gigi a fistful of tissues. Gigi buried her face in the pink, scented puffs and sobbed, "I just need to go home. I just need to go *home*."

"What's your last name, doll?"

"Prince."

Mrs. Meara nodded, tapped at her keyboard, and dialed the phone. "Mrs. Prince," she said. "Your daughter wants to speak to you. Hold on, please." Mrs. Meara passed Gigi the phone.

"What's wrong?" Gigi's mother asked immediately, sounding alarmed.

"Nothing," Gigi said, sniffing. "Can you come get me?"

"But it's Ms. Marian's day to carpool."

"That's *why* I need you to come get me," Gigi said, with fresh tears. "I can't deal with Finn. Please, Mama, please come get me."

There was a pause. Then her mom said, "Okay. I'm on my way."

Gigi sat on a bench in the office, alternately crying and sipping the Dixie cup of water Mrs. Meara foisted on her after she'd gotten off the phone. Her mother arrived fifteen minutes later. She thanked Mrs. Meara for taking care of Gigi and then ushered her out to the car, rubbing her shoulder as they walked. This made Gigi cry even harder.

Gigi waited for her mother to ask her what was wrong, but she didn't, and Gigi didn't offer any answers.

Instead she said, "I can't play in Sunday's game now."

"Oh?" her mother replied.

"Coach said I couldn't if I left practice. Team rules."

Her mom nodded. "Makes sense."

"I guess so." Gigi rubbed at her red, raw eyes. "Daddy's going to be disappointed in me."

"Why's that?"

"Because he was looking forward to seeing me play," Gigi said. "He told me that."

Her mother chuckled. "Daddy's looking forward to seeing *you*. There's a difference."

"I can't wait to see him too," Gigi said. "I really, really miss him, Mama."

"I know," she said. "I do too. But it's only a few more days, and then he'll be back. At least for a little while."

Her mother pulled into the driveway, put the car in park, and turned to Gigi. "Look," she said. "I know things haven't been easy, what with your dad out of town and the stuff with Finn. But your dad *is* coming home, and Finn *is* still your best friend. Even if you're having a few bumps in the road, you can't erase the kind of history that the two of you share."

Gigi nodded.

"But . . . ?" her mother prompted.

"But it doesn't feel that way," Gigi said. "I mean, right this second? It just really hurts."

They went into the house, and her mother put water on for tea. She didn't even have to ask Gigi if she wanted any; she just *knew*.

"Aren't you going to ask me why I had you pick me up?" Gigi asked, cradling her hot mug on the family room couch.

Her mom shrugged. "I figured you'd tell me when you were ready."

Gigi recounted her earlier conversation with Kendall. Then she told her mom about what had happened on the track.

"Hrm," her mom said.

"What?"

"I know I wasn't there," she said. "But it sounds like Finn apologized to you. More than once, yes?"

Gigi could feel her face flush hotly. "I guess, sort of."

"Not sort of," her mom corrected her. "You literally just told me that she apologized to you several times. So why didn't you want to accept?"

Now it was Gigi's turn to shrug.

"Sounds like you might be the one who owes *her* an apology now," her mother said. "But like I said, I wasn't there."

Gigi glared at her mother. "I hate it when you do that."

"Do what?"

"You know," she said. "Plant an idea in my head, but try to make it seem like it was my idea to begin with."

"*Me?*" her mother said, putting her hand over her heart. "Why, I would *never* do that to you, Gillian Gemma Prince." But the warm smile on her face contradicted the words completely.

"If you'll excuse me," Gigi said, "I have a phone call to make."

CHAPTER 16

"I mean it," said the voice on the other end of the line. "I'm totes glad you called."

It was Miranda, of course. Gigi had picked up the phone intending to call Finn, but in the end, she couldn't do it. In her head, she kept hearing all of the nasty things Kendall had reported to her in the lunch line today. Things Finn didn't exactly deny saying. Right now she felt like Finn was the *last* person she wanted to be speaking to.

Miranda, on the other hand . . . well, talking to Miranda was *fun*. And not only when they talked about whether an authentic fig marmalade or a trendier passion fruit gelée would make the best filling for their zeppole cupcake. The stories Miranda told her about her hippie dippy teachers and quirky fellow students at Fletcher Academy made Gigi laugh so hard her stomach cramped up. And Miranda couldn't stop giggling herself when Gigi told her all about the French Club.

After a while, Gigi found herself sharing all kinds of things with Miranda—how she felt about her dad being away, what it was like to find out that Finley had been talking about her behind her back, and even her disappointment at not being able to play in Sunday's soccer opener.

"I can be a total disaster on the field," Gigi confessed. "But I do try pretty hard. Most of the time."

"You know, if you really want to play," Miranda said, "you should tell your coach that. Maybe she'd make an exception."

Gigi considered this. Did she really want to play? Badly enough to beg Coach for another chance?

Even though her mom said her dad didn't care one way or another, Gigi knew how much he'd always enjoyed going to her games. One time, when she and Finn were still in the intramural league, he told her that he wished his job was flexible enough that he could volunteer to be a coach.

Plus, Gigi had gotten marginally better at the game as a Sterling Songbird. Soccer might not be her thing, but she had to admit to herself that she got better at it the more she tried.

"Is that a totally crazy idea?" Miranda asked. "Petitioning the coach to let you play?"

"No," Gigi said. "It's a really good idea. In fact, I might just do that."

The next day, Gigi's mother once again drove her into school early. Gigi had told her that she needed to track Coach down before homeroom, to ask if there was any way she could play in Sunday's game. The truth was, she could have found Coach after school—the varsity team practiced on the field the days the JV team had off—but getting her mom to drive offered the added bonus of not taking the bus with Finn.

When she arrived at Sterling, insulated lunch bag clutched firmly in her hand, Gigi went straight to the front office. Mrs. Meara was behind the desk, wearing a loud, rainbow-striped sweater and munching loudly on some sort of granola bar. "How ya doing, doll?" she said through a mouthful of granola. "Feeling any better?"

"Yes, thanks," Gigi said. "I'm looking for Coach Wedderburn. Do you know where she is before first bell?"

"She's usually in the weight room, but let me check," Mrs. Meara said. She tapped at her keyboard with her two pointer fingers, which were long and painted emerald green. *Probably for St. Patrick's Day,* Gigi thought. "Yep, she's in the weight room."

Gigi hadn't known that Sterling Middle School even had a weight room. She asked Mrs. Meara where it was.

"It's that annex off the gym," she said. "Not the closet. Or the other closet. The room in between. There should be a sign."

Gigi thanked Mrs. Meara and set off in search of the weight room. It did not, as Mrs. Meara said, have a sign. But the two closets did, and she figured that the unmarked door between GYM CLOSET and JANITOR CLOSET led to the weight room. She knocked and waited.

"It's open!" Gigi heard Coach call out. She took a deep breath and entered the room slowly, not sure what she'd find on the other side of the door.

The space was bigger than she expected. Its floor was covered in dense foam tiles that fit together like puzzle pieces, and there were several machines with various levers and pulleys dotted throughout the room. It smelled like a less-strong version of their practice pinafores.

Coach was standing in front of a wall of mirrors, a ginormous spray bottle of glass cleaner in one hand

178

and a thick wad of newspaper in the other.

"Feeling better, Prince?" she asked, not bothering to turn around.

"Much," Gigi said. She made eye contact with Coach in the mirror. "In fact, I wanted to ask you if there was any way I could still play in Sunday's game."

"You *want to* ask me, or you *are* asking me?" Coach shot back, scrubbing the mirror down with the wadded-up paper.

"I am asking," Gigi said. "My dad—he's been in Europe for weeks, but he's flying home on Saturday, and he's really been looking forward to seeing me play."

"Huh." Coach turned around to face Gigi. "You want me to let you play for your dad?"

"Yes," Gigi said. "Well, and for me too."

Coach surveyed Gigi intently. "Go on."

"Look, I know I missed yesterday's practice," Gigi said. "And I shouldn't have left. I was just having this really, really bad day and—"

"Stop right there," Coach said. "'Having a bad day' isn't a valid reason for skipping practice. We all have them. Doesn't give us the freedom to bail on our commitments, does it?"

"No."

"I told you before you walked off the field that if you didn't practice, you couldn't play," Coach said. "So you tell me. Why should I break that rule for you?"

Gigi shifted nervously from one foot to the other. She had a pretty good feeling that whatever answer she gave Coach shouldn't include the words "my dad." Maybe asking her for a second chance wasn't such a good idea after all.

"Say what you're thinking," Coach encouraged.

"I know I'm, like, the worst player on your team," Gigi said finally. "And to be perfectly honest, sometimes I don't even *like* playing. It's just this thing I've done for years. But lately I've been trying out all of these new . . . I don't even know what you'd call them. Hobbies? Interests? And I haven't been so good at them either. At least with soccer, I can see that when I'm trying, I am actually okay, you know? And I think, maybe I can keep getting better. I want to keep trying."

Coach nodded, as if Gigi had given her the correct answer. "Okay. Bring your gear tomorrow and plan to stay after school. You practice with my varsity team, and I'll let you play on Sunday."

"Really?" Gigi said.

"Really," Coach repeated. "But I need to see you

putting in real effort the entire time. Practice, the game itself . . . You check out even for thirty seconds, and I promise you I will bench your behind."

"Thank you," Gigi said, her voice barely above a whisper. She had the sudden urge to hug Coach Wedderburn but was fairly certain that Coach Wedderburn wasn't much of a hugger.

"Coach?"

"Yes?"

"Can I ask why you're rubbing old newspaper over the mirrors?"

Coach laughed. "Rags leave streaks on the glass. This doesn't." She pointed the newspaper ball towards the clock. "You better get on to homeroom. First bell's going to ring in a few minutes."

Gigi practically skipped down the hall. She couldn't wait to call Miranda after school to let her know that her idea had worked. Well, after her private clarinet lesson, that is. She wondered if she'd get home early enough to try to Skype with her dad. Italy was six hours ahead of Delaware, which meant as long as she got in by five she should be able to catch him. But even if she couldn't, she was going to get to see him in two more days.

Everything, it seemed, was coming up Gigi.

• • •

"Ow!" Gigi cried. "Ow, ow, ow!"

"What?" Ms. Panettiere said. "What is it?"

It was after school, and Gigi was in the music room. After learning about the clarinet—its different parts, and the perfect mouth position and breath, she had finally played her very first note.

It had not gone as well as she had hoped.

"My lip!" Gigi said. "I think I broke it."

"I doubt that," the teacher said. "Here, let me see."

Ms. P examined her lip, then reached for the clarinet. "I think it may be the reed."

"What do you mean?" Gigi ran her finger over the lump that was starting to form on her bottom lip. "Something's stuck," she said.

Ms. P said, "I believe you may have a splinter in your lip."

"A splinter?"

She nodded. "From the reed."

Of course there's a reed splinter in my bottom lip, Gigi thought. *Of course.*

Ms. P started to disassemble one of the clarinets. "Let me put these away and get you down to the nurse's office. I'm pretty sure Mrs. Fausnaugh stays until four."

The nurse was locking her door, clearly ready to

leave for the day, when Gigi and Ms. P reached her office. By that time, Gigi's lip lump had grown to the size of a pea.

"We are so sorry to bother you," Ms. Panettiere said, "but we have a bit of a splinter situation." Then she mouthed, "It's in her lip," tapping her own bottom lip for emphasis.

"This," Mrs. Fausnaugh said, "I gotta see."

After numbing her lip with ice and cleaning the area with some alcohol on a cotton pad, Mrs. Fausnaugh held a magnifying glass over the lump. "Looks like it's sticking out just a bit. I might be able to massage it out. Oh, man, I have never seen anything like this in my entire life."

Gigi thought, *This cannot get any worse.*

When Gigi's mother picked her up from school, she took one look at her face and said, "Dare I ask?"

"Lip splinter," Gigi explained. "Translation: me and the clarinet get along about as well as me and knitting needles."

"Oh, Gigi," her mom said. "I know you want to be good at everything, but—"

"I'd settle for being good at *something*," Gigi interrupted.

"Uh, you're good at a lot of somethings," her mother said. "Cooking, baking, acting, party planning, wardrobe styling . . ."

"Those things don't count," Gigi protested.

"Why not?"

"Because I love doing all of them."

Her mother shook her head. "So let me get this straight. Being good at something only counts if you don't love the thing that you're good at?"

"That's not what I meant."

"So what *did* you mean?"

"I don't know!" Gigi said. "It just seems like I'm really bad at all of this new stuff I've been trying out. Like maybe the only things I'll ever be good at are the things I'm *already* good at. Am I making any sense?"

Her mother didn't respond right away. Then she said, "I think you're being really hard on yourself. In the past two weeks, I've watched you not only step outside of your comfort zone, but move to a whole new area code. And no matter how you feel about all of these experiments, I want you to know that I am so incredibly proud of you, Gillian Gemma Prince. You are my amazerful daughter, and I would like you even if you weren't my kid."

Those were some of the best compliments Gigi had

ever received, from her mother or anyone else. She reached over the emergency brake and hugged her mom tightly. Then she said, "Let's try to remember this moment the next time I do something wrong, okay?"

"Deal."

CHAPTER 17

During Friday's morning announcements, Gigi's drama teacher, Mrs. Dempsey, came over the PA system. Gigi sat up rigidly. This was the moment she'd been waiting for the entire school year.

"Each spring, Sterling Middle School mounts a musical," Mrs. Dempsey said. "This year, after much deliberation, the show that's been selected is—drum roll, please!"

There was a light click, and then a tinny, garbled drum roll rumbled from the classroom's speakers—most likely a sound effect from someone's iPod. Then, the dramatic reveal: *The Wizard of Oz.*"

Gigi jumped in her seat, knocking her backpack off the attached desk. She didn't care; she could barely contain her excitement. *The Wizard of Oz!* How many times had she and Finley watched the movie, belted out "Over the Rainbow," dressed up like their childhood hero, Dorothy Gale? Instinctively, Gigi looked towards Finn's assigned seat, two rows over. But Finn's head was bent over a book, and Gigi couldn't even catch her eye.

"Auditions will be held this Tuesday in the auditorium," Mrs. Dempsey said over the speaker. "Be prepared to read lines and sing a song of your choice— anything *but* 'Over the Rainbow,' please."

Gigi barely heard this part of the announcement. All she could think was that the old Eff and Gee would've been squealing *together*, no matter how many seats separated them physically. The fact that Gigi couldn't share her absolute delight with her (former?) BFF deflated her joy like a popped balloon.

And yet . . . Gigi wondered if the middle school musical could be the thing that reunited Eff and Gee. *The Wizard of Oz*—what were the odds? Of course, they couldn't *both* play Dorothy, but seeing that they were only in sixth grade, it was highly unlikely either of them would be cast in the role anyway. With her long red curls, Gigi was way more likely to nab the part of Glinda the Good Witch. Was Lauren Avila into theater? Maybe she could be the Wicked Witch of the East, and get a house dropped on her in Act One.

Gigi instantly felt ashamed. She didn't actually dislike Lauren Avila, and she certainly didn't want anything bad to happen to her—she just really missed her friend. It was high time she stopped blaming Lauren for what happened between her and Finley, Gigi thought. After all, she knew it wasn't Lauren's fault. Lauren was simply a supercool soccer star who had a lot in common with Gigi's BFF. It's not like she had *forced* Finn to bail on Gigi over and over again. No, those were decisions Finn made for *herself.*

For the rest of homeroom, Gigi kept stealing glances in Finn's direction, but she never once looked up from her book. She refused to make eye contact with Gigi at lunch too. They still sat at the same table, but they'd barely spoken to each other all week.

Today was the worst, though. Today Finn wolfed down her PB&J in four bites, bit into a big, juicy apple, and excused herself to go work on some extra-credit assignment in the library. Their entire circle was dumbfounded.

"What is this nonsense?" Kendall practically hissed the minute Finn was out of earshot. "You told me the two of you were okay."

"Well, I guess I lied!" Gigi snapped. "You didn't help, you know. Why did you have to tell me that Finn was talking about me to Katie anyway?"

"You did what?" Katie said, her head whipping in Kendall's direction. "You promised me you wouldn't say anything!"

"GUYS!" Maggie yelled, hitting the table with the heel of her hand. "Enough! We are all girlfriends—emphasis on the *friends* part. We do not act like this to each other. Katie, you shouldn't have been gossiping."

Kendall stuck her tongue out in Katie's direction.

"And *you*," Maggie said to Kendall, "shouldn't have been trying to start a fire."

"Thank you," Gigi said with a toss of her hair.

Maggie's eyes narrowed slightly. "Don't think you're off the hook, Gigi."

"What did *I* do?"

"Whatever this thing is between you and Finley, it has to stop," she said. "Look what it's doing to us!" Her voice lowered until it was barely above a whisper. "We're starting to act like . . . like the mean girls."

"We are nothing like the mean girls," Gigi protested. "We're just girls, dealing with some stuff."

"Then deal with it," Maggie said firmly. "Don't pretend like nothing's wrong. Clearly things are wrong. And the longer you and Finn avoid dealing with them, the harder it's going to be on the rest of us.

189

"Frankly," she continued, "I think the two of you are being a little selfish. And I, for one, don't want any part of your drama."

Maggie stood up from the table, stuffing the rest of her lunch back into its bag.

"Where are you going?" Katie asked.

She shrugged. "I don't know. But I can't stay here. I've lost my appetite."

"Talk about drama," Gigi muttered as Maggie stomped away from the table.

Kendall shook her head. "Nice, Gigi. Real nice." Then she too packed up her things and headed for the door. Katie mouthed "I'm sorry" to Gigi, then grabbed her stuff and followed after Kendall, leaving Gigi all alone at their end of the lunch table.

Gigi was floored. What had just happened? *How* had it happened? She was pretty sure people had started to stare.

Her first instinct was to fake an upset stomach and go for the early dismissal. But if Gigi did that, she couldn't practice with the varsity team after school, and then Coach would never let her play in Sunday's game. Plus, if she went home sick, there was no way her mom would let Miranda spend the night.

No, Gigi would have to stick it out, no matter how

embarrassed she was. At least for now. She opened her backpack, pulled out a loose-leaf sheet of paper, and wrote the words *I refuse to be a sad mopey* over and over again while she finished up her lunch.

After the final bell, Gigi decided to skip the locker room and change in the second-floor girls' bathroom instead. It was going to be weird enough that a sure-to-be-benched-on-Sunday sixth grader from the JV team would be practicing with the older girls; she didn't want to deal with the pre-practice locker room awkwardness to boot.

She went back downstairs to her locker and shoved her backpack and duffle bag into the tiny metal space. Then she headed out to the field, feeling even more self-conscious than she had at lunch.

Let's just get this over with, she thought.

"Hey, Coach," Gigi said almost shyly.

"Prince, you made it!" Coach bellowed when she saw her. "I wasn't sure you would."

"I said I was coming. So here I am."

Coach Wedderburn nodded. "Varsity practice is a little different from what you're used to," she said. "Be prepared to run. A lot."

Girls spilled out onto the field, but Gigi kept her focus

on her feet. Until, that is, she heard a familiar voice.

Finley?

Gigi's head popped up. Sure enough, Finn was standing ten feet away, chatting with Lauren Avila and a few other eighth graders. She was wearing her normal practice gear; clearly she wasn't here only to hang out with her friends. Gigi's cheeks began to burn. When had Finn started practicing with the varsity team? And why hadn't she said anything to Gigi about it?

Their eyes met briefly. Finley's face scrunched up in confusion.

Gigi shrugged and mouthed, "Long story."

Finn closed her eyes and shook her head, much like she did when Logan was annoying her and she pretended she could blink him away.

Was this what it had come to? Had Finn started to regard her in the same way she did her hyperbratty little brother?

As for the running: Coach Wedderburn wasn't kidding. They did the same number of laps as the JV team, but Coach had them alternate between three-quarter pace running, jogging, sprinting, and walking. Every time Coach blew her whistle, they moved to the next phase of the sequence, hitting all four in a single lap. Before she started, Gigi thought that having walking breaks would make it easier, but going from fast to medium to superfast to superslow and then back up to fast again caused Gigi's legs to ache in a way she never knew was possible.

When the laps were completed, Coach gave them a five-minute water break, and then it was on to drills. In some ways, the drills the varsity girls did were way more basic than the ones Coach had the JV team run. But, as Gigi soon realized, the reason for this was because Coach demanded precision.

"It's all about control, ladies," Coach barked. "I want to see controlled passing, controlled turns, controlled shooting. Remember, *you* need to have command over the ball—you can't let that ball control you."

Drills lasted for half an hour, after which Coach gave them another five-minute water break. Then she declared it was time for one-on-ones and started pairing off the girls.

Oh no, Gigi thought.

But, *oh yes*, Coach put the two JV girls together. Finn didn't protest, but she didn't look happy about it either. Gigi wished the ground would open up and swallow her whole.

The first game they played was Shadow. Gigi groaned inwardly. She hated this game, in which one player had to copy the other player's moves until the first player could completely fake the second player out. Then they switched roles, with the follower becoming the leader.

"You want to start?" Finley asked.

"Whatever," Gigi said. "I'll go get the ball."

"No ball," Finn said. "Just us."

Coach blew her whistle, and Gigi pretended to drive a ball down the length of the field. Finn anticipated her every move. Of course she did. They used to share the same brain.

As a final attempt to fake Finn out, Gigi launched into a scissors move. Only she overshot the imaginary ball completely, lost control of her legs, and landed hard smack on her tailbone.

"Ouch," Finn said, extending a hand. "You okay?"

"Like you care," Gigi muttered. She struggled to her feet on her own, as if Finn wasn't offering the assist.

Finley's jaw dropped slightly, and she stared at Gigi in mild disbelief. Then she snapped her mouth shut until her lips were a tight line of anger.

"Are we practicing or what?" Gigi asked.

"Fine," Finn said. "My turn."

Regardless of how she was feeling about Finley, Gigi couldn't help but admire her footwork on the field.

She'd often thought Finn didn't play soccer so much as she danced through it. Her feet were fast and never stopped moving, yet there was nothing haphazard about anything she did. It was all about precision. Gigi, of course, couldn't keep up, but she never stopped trying.

The next game involved five girls working together, one on each corner of a large square demarcated by mini orange cones, with the fifth standing in the middle. Each of the corner girls had a ball, and they'd drive it towards the center girl, who would run up and try to defend. They weren't actually supposed to stop or steal the ball, just close up the space. After they met, the monkey in the middle would move to the next girl, while the one with the ball dribbled it back to the corner. Every forty-five seconds or so, Coach would blow the whistle, and the middle girl would switch out for a corner post.

Of course, Gigi *would* end up in a group with Finn and Lauren Avila. She tried not to resent the fact that, even during a punishing practice like this, Lauren looked like a model from a *Seventeen* photo shoot.

What's worse was that it was so clear to Gigi that Finn fit in Lauren's world now. She was a polished, confident athlete—quite a contrast to the hot mess that Gigi often felt like inside.

When practice was over, Gigi skipped the last five-minute water break. She wanted to get off the field as fast as possible. Miranda would be coming over around six, and she needed to shower and clean her room. Plus, she thought if she was quick enough, she and her mom would avoid running into Ms. Marian in the parking lot. That would only lead to questions about why they hadn't worked out a carpool, and Gigi didn't feel like explaining to either of them that she and Finn didn't know they'd be at the same practice.

She hadn't gotten far when Coach called her over. For a second, Gigi thought she was going to be told that she still couldn't play in Sunday's game. Instead, Coach actually *complimented* her.

"You did good out there," she said with a smile. "I saw you keeping pace. Not easy with these girls. I'm proud of you, Prince."

Gigi's face split in a grin she couldn't hide even if she'd wanted to. "Thanks, Coach. Does this mean I can play?"

"I'll see you Sunday."

Gigi sprinted for her locker, the sweetness of success temporarily melting away her muscle fatigue. Then she darted for the parking lot. Everything came to a screeching halt when she saw Ms. Marian and her mother leaning against the side of Ms. Marian's Jeep, talking and laughing like everything was business as usual.

"I didn't know you were practicing with the varsity team too!" Ms. Marian said. "I would've offered you a ride."

"It was just this once," Gigi explained. "To make up for a practice I missed earlier in the week."

"Oh, I see."

"Well, we have to get going," Gigi's mom said. "I need to a run a couple of errands, and Gigi's friend from cooking class is coming over tonight." She hugged Ms. Marian and said they needed to plan a scrapbooking date soon.

"I should have you all over for dinner next week," Ms. Marian said. "Gigi, maybe you and Finn could whip up dessert together."

Without thinking, Gigi rolled her eyes.

"Hey," her mother said sharply. "Not nice."

Ms. Marian's brow furrowed. "What's going on, Gee? I don't mean to pry, but Finley has been moping around the house all week, and I couldn't help but notice you haven't been calling or coming over as much."

"You'll have to ask Finn about that," Gigi said flatly.

"Gigi!" her mother exclaimed.

"Well, it's true!" Gigi said. "She's the one spreading rumors about me. She's even turning our friends against me! Ask her about what happened at lunch today, Ms. Marian. Just ask her."

Ms. Marian's furrow turned into an outright frown. "I'll do that."

Gigi's mother started to apologize on her behalf, but Gigi cut her off. "Mama, stop. Please. I know you always think these things are my fault, but it's not just me. Finn's hurt my feelings too. All the times she's blown off our plans, those things she said to Katie, how she won't even look me in the eye anymore . . ." Gigi could feel the threat of tears but refused to cry. "Can we please just go now? Please?"

The two moms exchanged looks that Gigi pretended not to see. "Go on, get in the car," Gigi's mother said. As Gigi buckled herself into the backseat, she could see that her mom had some hushed consultation with Ms. Marian. Then there was another hug and a wave good-bye.

Gigi's mom didn't say much as they drove to the bank, the gas station, and the grocery store. She did ask Gigi to pick up some more flour and any other baking supplies that had been depleted during the cupcake bake-off prep, but otherwise they barely spoke. In the bakery section, Gigi spied boxes of mini cannoli shells, which she immediately added to the cart. She still wanted to remake the recipe from the batter disaster, and the shells gave her a great idea for the topping.

Just over an hour later, they finally headed for home. Gigi was surprised when, out of nowhere, her mother apologized to her.

"I can't stop thinking about what you said to Ms. Marian," her mother began. "About me always thinking things are your fault. I don't, you know. And I'm really, really sorry I made you feel that way."

"Thanks," Gigi said.

"Do you want to tell me about what happened at lunch today?"

"Not especially."

"Is there anything you *do* want to tell me?"

"Actually, yeah," Gigi said. "They finally announced the spring musical! It's going to be—get this—*The Wizard of Oz*. Auditions are on Tuesday."

"That's great, Gee!" her mom exclaimed. "You and Finn must be so excited."

"*I* am excited," Gigi said. "But Finn looked like she couldn't care less. And Mama, I'll be honest—when Mrs. Dempsey made the announcement, I thought it was, like, *fate*." She sighed and looked out the window. "I just have to accept the fact that Finley doesn't want to be my friend right now."

At that exact moment, as they turned onto their street, Gigi could see a familiar figure boarding a bright red bicycle in the driveway.

Finn.

"Looks like you might be wrong," Gigi's mother said. She waved to Finn, who offered a halfhearted smile and waved back. "Hey, Ms. Nancy," Finn said.

"Hello, Finley," Gigi's mom said. "It's so good to see you. Grab a bag of groceries and come on in."

Finn and Gigi exchanged looks. Their silent conversation went something like this:

FINN: *Do you want me to come in?*

GIGI: *Only if you want to.*

FINN: *I asked you first.*

GIGI: *Fine, come in.*

The girls helped Gigi's mom bring the groceries inside and then headed up to Gigi's room. They stood facing each other, Finn munching on a cuticle and Gigi tugging on a loose red curl.

"What are you doing here?" Gigi asked.

"Trying to talk to you."

"So, talk."

Neither of them said anything.

"Look," Gigi said after a long, awkward silence. "I'm sorry your mom made you come over here, but—"

"This wasn't my mom's idea," Finn said.

"Well, then why—"

"Because I don't like this," she interrupted. "Dude, you're supposed to be my best friend."

"And you're supposed to be mine," Gigi said. "But it sure doesn't feel that way lately, does it?"

"No," Finn replied in a small, quiet voice. "I guess it doesn't."

Finn plopped down on the shaggy rug. Then she gestured for Gigi to sit too. Gigi ignored this and remained standing.

"It's just that you've been acting so jealous," Finn said. "It's really—"

"Annoying," Gigi interjected, crossing her arms over her chest. "I know. You told me that last week, remember?"

Finley tucked her legs up under her chin and rested her head on her knees. "I guess I don't understand why me being friends with Lauren Avila is such a big deal to you."

"It's a big deal because you made it one," Gigi said. "Like that messed-up trip to the mall. *You* invited *me*, remember? And then you couldn't even be bothered to talk to me. I spent the entire time chatting up Lauren's *mother*."

Finn opened her mouth to protest, but Gigi threw up her hand in the universal sign for STOP.

"It's true, Finley," Gigi insisted. "You asked me to come. You said you wanted me to get to know Lauren better. And then you did everything you could to make me feel like I wasn't even there. Plus, what about all that stuff you said to Katie?"

"I already apologized for that!"

Gigi snorted. "Well, it didn't stop you from dissing me in homeroom and at lunch."

"Gee, I'm sorry you feel like, I don't know, like I don't like you anymore or something. But it's not true. It's not! And the way you're acting, it's a little . . ." She trailed off.

"A little what?" Gigi challenged. "Go ahead, say it!"

Before Finley could respond, the doorbell rang below. A quick glance at the clock revealed that it was just after five thirty. "She's early," Gigi said aloud.

"Who's early?" Finley asked.

"Miranda."

"Who?"

"Miranda," Gigi repeated. "From cooking class."

"Weird Girl?"

"I told you," Gigi said. "She's my *friend*."

"Since when?"

"Since why do you even care? She's my friend, and she's coming over to spend the night, and you—*you're not invited*."

The harsh words seemed to startle Gigi even as they came out of her own mouth.

"Fine!" Finley said, springing to her feet. "I don't want to be invited to your stupid weird sleepover anyway. And guess what? I don't want to share my birthday with you either."

Gigi stepped backwards as if Finn had slapped her across the face. It all started to make sense. No wonder it had been so hard for them to pin down a theme in the first place. Finley must've been trying to stall until she could figure a way to wiggle out of the party altogether.

One hot tear slid down Gigi's cheek. She wiped it away quickly and said, "Okay, then. It's decided. No more double birthday parties. And definitely no more best friendship."

Finn nodded. "Sounds about right."

"You can leave now," Gigi said. *"Dude."*

Gigi watched Finn stomp out of the room, her blond hair streaking behind her in a golden blur. She couldn't catch her breath.

Did that really just happen?

"Finley, wait!" she called after her (former?) best friend, and started to run after her. Only it was too late—Finn was gone, and Gigi had run smack into Miranda.

Their foreheads collided with a dull *thunk*, and Gigi bounced backwards.

"Ow!" Miranda said, rubbing her right eyebrow. "What was *that* all about?"

Gigi couldn't speak. She pressed the heels of her hands over her eyes and fought the urge to howl.

"Whoa," Miranda said. "Are you okay?"

"I'm fine," Gigi replied, even though she was anything but. "Just been a long day." She dropped her arms to her sides and forced herself to smile.

"Don't do that," Miranda said. "First of all, that smile is wicked creepy. Fact: most fake smiles are. But also, it is one hundred percent A-okay for you to say, 'No, Miranda, I am not okay. In fact, I am the very opposite of okay.' Because clearly you are so not okay."

Miranda's directness was one of the things that had made Gigi think she was sort of weird to begin with.

Now, she realized, it was one of the things she liked best about her.

So they talked. Once again, Gigi marveled at how easy it was to tell Miranda anything. She wasn't judgey, like Kendall could sometimes be, and she wasn't neutrally detached, like Katie almost always was. Miranda listened, plain and simple. She asked questions too, but they weren't like Maggie's attempts to shift the conversation to another topic entirely.

When she finished, Miranda said, "So let's recap. On the one hand, you kicked butt at soccer practice and got props from your coach, your mom apologized to *you* for making *you* feel bad, your dad's coming home tomorrow after being gone forever, and your supercool new friend is at your house, ready to throw down with you in the kitchen. All good, yes?"

Gigi nodded.

"On the other hand, we have the whole girls-abandoning-you-at-lunch thing and the blowup you just had with Blondie. That's the not-so-good."

Gigi nodded again.

"I'm not going to lie," Miranda said. "The not-so-good stuff is pretty awful. But the good stuff is pretty amazing. And there is definitely a lot more of the good going on right now, you know? Plus, I have to say, I don't think you and Finley are really Donesville. I mean, just look at your room." Miranda extended one hand and gestured to the Wall like a game-show hostess. "Seriously. It's like something out of a movie."

But Gigi didn't want to look at the Wall right now. She didn't want to be reminded of how different things had become.

"There's no time for looking," Gigi said. "Now, we must bake."

CHAPTER 18

"Well, what do we have here?" Chef Angela asked, examining the two cupcakes Gigi and Miranda had put before her.

Cupcake Number One was the zeppole-inspired one that Miranda had dreamed up. Vanilla, filled with a simple but oh-so-rich Italian pastry cream and topped with a tall swirl of whipped cream frosting and a miniature zeppole.

It wasn't as splashy looking as Cupcake Number Two, which was a revamped version of the cannoli cupcake Gigi had started with. Miranda's mastery of baking ratios had taken the thing from the batter disaster and turned it into something truly special: a light ricotta cupcake filled with a mini-chocolate-chip-speckled cannoli cream. It used the same whipped cream frosting as the zeppole cupcake, only instead of a little doughnut, it was topped with chopped pistachios and half of a mini cannoli shell.

Chef Angela took a bite of the zeppole cupcake first and chewed thoughtfully. "This is OMG good," she said. "You girls are major-league impressive."

Gigi beamed. "Now try the other one."

They watched Chef Angela lift the cannoli cupcake to her nose, breathing in its creamy, nutty scent. Slowly she turned the cupcake in her hand, as if she was looking for the perfect place to take the first bite. Then she peeled down a section of the wrapper, exposing some of the cake, and bit in.

Chef Angela's eyes closed almost immediately, and before she said a single word, she went back in for a second bite.

They held their collective breath as Chef Angela leaned in for a third bite. Before she sank her teeth in again, she turned to the girls and said, "Y'all know this confection is perfection, right?"

Miranda and Gigi grinned at each other while Chef Angela ate the rest of the cupcake. When she was finished, she said, "Tell me. What made you turn a cannoli into a cupcake?"

"It was Gigi's idea," Miranda said. "Her dad's been in Italy on business. She made the first version all by herself."

"But it was awful," Gigi added quickly. "Miranda totally fixed the cupcake part. She's, like, a baking wizard."

Miranda shook her head. "The flavor is what makes it, though, and that's all Gigi."

"Sounds like this was a true team effort," Chef Angela cut in. "Bravo, girls. I wouldn't change a thing."

Gigi and Miranda went outside to tell their moms the good news, and to offer Miranda's mom a cupcake, since she hadn't gotten to taste one yet. Her mom took a dainty, birdlike nibble and said, "Mmm, that *is* good!" She took a much larger second bite.

"My mom's not crazy about sugar," Miranda explained. "But two bites means she *really* likes it."

The girls said their good-byes, as Gigi and her mother were off to the airport to pick up Gigi's dad.

"Good luck tomorrow," Miranda said. "Call me after the game?"

"Definitely."

Gigi felt squirmy on the ride to the airport. She'd worn a denim mini over sparkly black leggings, but the leggings were too warm for this particular spring day and the sparkly threads were making her skin itch. She kept checking the small cooler she'd stocked with extra cannoli cupcakes to make sure they were okay, but her constant fussing irritated her mother, who kept saying, "Every time you open it, you let the cold air out and the warm air in!" When they hit a bumper-to-bumper traffic jam in a construction zone seven miles from their exit, Gigi thought the frustration might make her head literally explode.

Finally—finally!—they reached the Philadelphia International Airport. Between the flight's slight delay and the unexpected snarl of traffic, Gigi and her mother managed to arrive just after her dad cleared customs. Not five minutes later, he emerged from the sliding doors with a cart of luggage and a face-splitting grin.

Gigi bolted from the car and took a running jump into her father's arms. He wrapped her up in a big bear hug and spun her around a little. "How's my girl?" he asked after planting a kiss on the top of her head. Then he set Gigi down gently and turned to her mom. "How's my other girl?"

A big mama-jama smooch came next; Gigi averted her eyes accordingly. After all, no one likes seeing their parents make out *at all*, let alone in public.

They loaded her dad's luggage into the trunk and started on the half-hour ride home. He told them about the flight, which would've been uneventful if the guy seated next to him hadn't started buzz-saw snoring halfway home.

"I have to tell you, Gee, it was so loud, even my earplugs didn't block it out," he said. "Wait! I recorded some on my phone."

He played the sound clip. Sure enough, every three seconds an enormous, guttural snore erupted, each one making Gigi giggle that much harder.

She opened the cooler and extracted one of the cannoli cupcakes. Then she handed it to her dad in the front seat. "You have to try these, Daddy. Chef Angela said it was 'confection perfection.'"

Gigi's dad took a sloppy bite. "Aww, man," he said. "That is one heck of a cupcake."

"Does it taste like a real Italian cannoli?" Gigi asked.

"The realest."

Gigi peppered her dad with all of the questions she hadn't gotten answered during their far-too-infrequent Skype calls. She wanted to know about the restaurants, the shops, and the fun things her father did while he was there.

He snorted. "Fun? What exactly do you think I do on these work trips, Gee?"

"Come on, Daddy," she said. "You must have had *some* fun. You were gone for weeks!"

"Well, I had a lot of fun picking out presents for you and your mom," he said. "Does that count?"

"Absolutely!"

Back at the house, Gigi's dad flopped into his favorite oversized, overstuffed easy chair and put his feet up on the ottoman. "It's so good to be home," he said. "But you know what's missing? A dog. In the movies, when a man comes home from a long business trip, he is almost always greeted by a big, fluffy dog."

"Are we getting a dog?" Gigi asked.

"No," her mother said. "We're not. George, stop giving her crazy ideas!"

"Having a family dog isn't so crazy," her dad said, giving Gigi a wink. "I hear they're great for teaching kids how to be responsible."

"Okay, fine," her mother said. "Gigi, if I gave you a choice between a dog and a cell phone, what—"

"Cell phone," Gigi interjected. "Hands down."

Gigi's mother gave her father a pointed look, which made him laugh.

"You're killing me, kiddo," he said. "We could have had a dog! Can you hand me that gray duffel?"

Gigi dragged the heavy duffel bag over to her dad. It was the one that folded up into a flat square for the trip over, then got stuffed with the presents he brought back from his travels.

The magical gray bag held all sorts of goodies: *Lebkuchen* gingerbread, carved wood Christmas ornaments, and shiny blue pottery with white polka dots from Germany; Karlovy Vary wafer cookies, a wooden marionette, and matching garnet rings from Prague; fancy balsamic vinegar, extra virgin olive oil, and tons of dried spices from Italy. But that wasn't all Gigi's father brought back; there were also leather gloves for her mother, millefiori earrings for Gigi, and Baci chocolates for both of them.

When Gigi had asked her dad to bring home a couple of things for an Italy-themed birthday party, she had no idea he'd go so over-the-top crazy. There were miniature flags, key chains, and patches. There were bags of Labello lip balms, Pocket Coffee chocolates, and an olivewood cheese board. There were pennants for Italian football teams ("That's what they call soccer, you know," he informed her), a blue ball emblazoned with ITALIA, and a sky blue jersey with the number twelve on the back.

"I thought you could give this to Finn to wear to the party," her dad said.

"Wow," Gigi said. "This is . . . really nice of you."

"You don't like the jersey?"

"It's not that!" Gigi said. "I just . . . Finn and I . . . I don't even know if there's going to *be* a party."

"That bad?" he said.

Gigi nodded.

"Is it something that can't be fixed? Something you don't *want* to fix?"

"I think I would want to fix it," Gigi said, "if I could figure out how. I don't really know when it got so bad in the first place."

Her father scratched at the five-o'clock shadow on his chin. "Want to walk me through it?"

Gigi told him everything, even the parts that made her look bad, like when she wouldn't accept Finn's apology. When she was finished, her dad said, "Have you tried hitting the reset button?"

"I don't understand."

"The reset button. Clear everything out. Forget everything that came before and start fresh."

Gigi cocked her head to one side. "Really? That's your big advice?"

"Okay, if you don't think that would work, then what will?"

She chewed on her bottom lip. It was a fair question.

"I don't know," she said. "Maybe nothing."

Her dad disagreed. "I don't buy it," he said. "You can resolve most interpersonal conflicts with increased communication. Have you increased your communication, Gigi?"

She wanted to say yes but couldn't. The truth was, she and Finn had been talking less and less—until they stopped talking altogether.

Her father said, "Well then, there you have it. Try increasing your communication, see what happens."

"But what if the other person doesn't want to be communicated with?" Gigi asked.

"Then it's not real communication," he said. "The kind I'm talking about requires both parties to listen as well as talk, to ask as well as answer. And if you can't get the other party to engage, then you're either not using the right communication technique, or they're uninterested in resolving the conflict to begin with. And if that's the case . . . well, honey, there really isn't much that you can do. But something tells me that's not the problem you're having with Finn."

Gigi nodded. Then she said, "Is this the kind of stuff you did when you were in Italy?"

"Sometimes."

"Then no wonder you didn't have any fun."

Gigi couldn't stop thinking about what her dad had said. How was she supposed to increase communication with someone who had outright told her that she didn't want to be her friend anymore? Of course, both of them had said things out of anger, and hurt.

For some reason, an image of Madame Fournier popped into her head. She kept thinking about how frustrated Madame got when Gigi couldn't understand that one sentence. She'd tried so hard to get her message across, but Gigi—and the rest of the club, for that matter—didn't know all of the words.

Maybe that's what I need, Gigi thought. *Maybe I just have to learn how to speak Finn.*

She looked around her room, her eyes first combing the massive collage that spanned the Wall. Evidence that she and Finn both had spoken the same language once. Then she looked down at the treasures her father had brought from Italy. She'd never gotten the chance to even tell Finn about her party idea, which was truly half her and half Gigi. Would it have made a difference?

Gigi had to find out. She picked up the phone and dialed Finn's number, but no one answered. She left a quick voice mail—"Hey, Eff, it's Gee. Can we talk? Call me . . . please."—and formulated her plan.

CHAPTER 19

The temperature plummeted nineteen degrees between Saturday and Sunday, which meant that most of the people watching the Sterling Middle School Songbirds play their first match were wearing coats and drinking hot chocolate that the band was selling for a dollar a cup.

"Smart kids," said Gigi's dad when they arrived and saw the long line snaking around the stand. "They're going to make boatloads of money today. Nance, you want a cocoa?"

Gigi joined her team, half of whom had already arrived and were jogging in place. Coach liked a good twenty-minute warm-up—knee raises, stretches, the whole nine. Gigi was jealous of the cocoa-fueled warming-up her parents were doing in the stands.

For the season opener, the Songbirds were set to play the Bunting Bumblebees. Gigi knew a couple of the girls from her time in the intramural league, and there was friendly waving. It seemed funny to Gigi how little real sports resembled the stuff you saw in the movies, where there seemed to be a lot of nail-biting and last-minute scoring to win the big game. Her soccer games tended to be way more boring.

When the girls were sufficiently warmed, Coach Wedderburn said, "All right, ladies. We're playing eight on eight today, which means two of you won't start. But everybody without an injury plays, so stay focused on the game and be prepared to get called in."

Coach started tapping girls' shoulders, to indicate they should take the field. In the end, Gigi was left standing with Kionna, who'd actually twisted her ankle earlier in the week and wasn't going to be playing anyway.

Gigi felt defeated as she and Ki took their seats on the cold metal bench.

"The longer you pout, the longer Coach will keep you benched," Ki advised. Gigi forced her face into a neutral position.

The first half rolled by uneventfully. There was scoring, of course, but it was almost like the teams were taking turns letting the other get the goal. Then, six minutes before halftime, the Songbirds woke up. Finley streaked across the field and shot a clean goal. Then she expertly stole the ball back from the Bumblebees and scored again. Just before the whistle, she made a third goal.

With the Songbirds firmly in the lead, Coach put Gigi in at midfield to start the second half. Gigi looked over to her dad and waved but saw that he and her mom were deep in conversation with Finley's parents. She was staring at them, trying to figure out what they were saying, when the first ball sailed right past her and into the Songbirds' goal.

"Look alive, Prince!" Coach bellowed. This, in addition to Gigi's benching during the first half of the game, made her a prime target for the Bumblebees. Gigi's defense was weak, and she let another player sail by, setting her up for the goal.

Coach called time. Gigi knew even before she said the words that she was getting pulled from the game.

But then Coach said, "Nguyen and Kirby, I want you to stick by Prince. The rest of you, keep doing what you're doing."

"You want us to guard defense?" Kelly Kirby asked.

Coach said, "You heard me."

Now that Gigi was protected by two seventh

graders, the Bumblebees seemed to lose interest in her. She spent the majority of the second half standing there, half wishing the ball would come to her and half praying that it wouldn't.

The Bumblebees scored again, tying the game seven to seven. Coach called the girls in for a huddle.

"They're putting too much heat on Stewart," she said. "Nguyen, you cover her. Kirby, you stay with Prince. Let's go, girls. I'm confident you can take the win."

This time, when the Bumblebees came after Finn, she had extra protection from Sunny Nguyen. But it still wasn't enough. The Bumblebees wouldn't let Finn anywhere near the goal. So instead of losing the ball, Finn aimed it right at Gigi.

Gigi's muscles took over when her brain froze at her only thought: *Oh no. I have the ball!*

She dribbled downfield, past the defensive line. A couple of Bumblebees stood right in her path! Gigi looked right. Kelly was in the clear. Gigi kicked. Kelly caught the pass and drove the ball farther towards the goal. By the time the Bumblebees figured out where the ball was, Kelly had passed it back to Finn, who sank the ball deep in the net.

221

GOAL!

The crowd went crazy. Everyone spilled out onto the field to congratulate Finn. Gigi half expected them to lift her up and crowd-surf her back to the bleachers. Either that or dump a cooler of Gatorade over her head.

Neither happened, of course. Instead, after the initial melee died down, the Songbirds lined up for the postgame handshake with the Bumblebees. Then people started to peel off and head home. Gigi was trying to find Finn when her dad came up from behind and startled her.

"Nice showing out there, kiddo," he said.

"You know, I wasn't half bad, was I?" Gigi smiled. She wasn't as *naturally* good at soccer as she was at some other things, but trying hard at something and not giving up, even when it was tough? That was pretty satisfying.

Gigi finally spotted Finn talking to her parents and Coach. She didn't want to interrupt, so she waited, watching. She was surprised to see Lauren Avila and her mother approach the group. Had they been in the stands the whole time?

Finn got lost in an ever-growing circle of admirers, and Gigi, still bruised from the game, gave up. She'd have to mend fences with Finn another day.

The game had wrapped around three thirty, too early for dinner but prime time for a snack. A lot of the kids headed to the Charcoal Pit for french fries and milkshakes, but to Gigi's relief, her parents were still full from all the cocoa they'd drank in the stands. They headed home instead.

At home, Gigi went up to her room to change. She thought about calling Miranda but figured it could wait. She didn't really feel like talking to anyone anyway.

It wasn't so long ago that Gigi had loved spending time in her room, what with her cozy loft bed, snuggles with Glamour Puss, and the Wall full of memories. But these days, Gigi felt like the Wall was fake. Maybe her dad was right about needing to hit the reset button. Maybe it was time to take down the Wall and start over fresh.

Gigi and her parents settled in to watch a DVD in the family room. Gigi's mom suggested *The Wizard of Oz*, to help Gigi prepare for her audition next week. They made a huge bowl of olive oil popcorn, which they shared back and forth while nestled under a large plaid blanket.

Dorothy had just landed in Oz when the doorbell

rang. Gigi's immediate thought was that Miranda had talked her mom into bringing her over to surprise Gigi. Only it wasn't Miranda on the other side of the door; it was Finn.

"Hi," she said, almost shyly. "Can I come in?"

"Who is it?" her mother asked.

"It's Finn," Gigi said.

"Finley!" Gigi's dad bellowed. "You're just in time. We're about to meet the Munchkins. Pull up a seat."

Gigi expected Finn to make some excuse or another. Instead she said, "That sounds great, Mr. George. Let me just call my mom and let her know."

Finley took her usual family movie night spot next to Gigi, pulled the blanket up to her chest, and said, "Can you please pass the popcorn, Ms. Nancy?"

Gigi was stunned. What was going on here? Why was Finn acting like nothing had ever happened? The whole thing left Gigi feeling slightly uneasy, even as she tried to settle into the familiar favorite.

They clapped at the end, just like they always did. Then Gigi's parents headed into the kitchen to order from their Chinese takeout place. "Want to stay for dinner, Finn?" Gigi's mom asked.

"Um . . ." Finn looked to Gigi as if seeking her approval.

"Yeah," Gigi said. "We're going to head up to my room now, okay?"

For some reason, Gigi thought she'd magically know what to say once they went upstairs, but of course she didn't. She offered up a lame "You played a really great game today."

"Thanks," Finn said. "That's actually why I came over."

"Oh?"

Finn took a deep breath and, with her eyes pasted on Gigi's penguin slipper socks, said, "Coach is moving me up to varsity starting next week."

"Whoa," Gigi said, duly impressed. "As a sixth grader?"

"Crazy, right? Lauren says there hasn't been a sixth grader on varsity—besides her and me, I mean—in at least five years."

"That's really awesome," Gigi said, and meant it.

"That's not even the best part. Coach is sending four girls to Florida this summer for an elite two-week training camp, and she said that *I'm* going to be one of them. It's in Orlando, Gee. Right near Disney World!"

Finn's happiness was contagious. Without even thinking, Gigi gave her a BFF hug.

"You totally deserve it," Gigi said.

"You mean it?"

"Yeah, of course."

"It's just . . ." Finley sighed. "I'm really sorry about what I said on Friday. I didn't mean it. I was just—"

"Mad," Gigi finished for her. "I know. Me too."

"Do you think we can get past this?" Finn asked.

Gigi paused. "Here," she said, "let me show you something."

Gigi went over to her closet and pulled out the plastic bin that held all of the things her dad had brought back from Italy. She sat on the floor and started laying them out around her in a half circle.

"What is all of this stuff?" Finn asked, smiling. She knelt down on the carpet with Gigi.

"This," Gigi said dramatically, "is our twelfth birthday party. Or at least what I hoped would be our twelfth birthday party."

Finn looked puzzled. "I don't get the theme. It's what? Soccer and lip gloss?"

"Lip balm," Gigi corrected. "And not just any lip balm. Special *Italian* lip balm." She waited patiently for Finn to make the connection. It took a few beats, but then her best friend's face lit up like a Christmas tree.

"Italy! The theme is Italy!"

"Yes!" Gigi said. "I want to create a mini Italian festival in the backyard, complete with soccer and spaghetti, football and fashion."

"A little bit me, a little bit you," Finn said.

"Exactly."

"You thought of this all on your own?" Finn asked.

"More or less. I realized it didn't have to be a big battle over who likes what. We just had to find something we both enjoyed. Equally. Even if it wasn't for the same reasons."

Finn smiled. "Does this mean we're not fighting anymore?"

"I don't know," Gigi teased. "What part are you going to try out for in *The Wizard of Oz*? Because if you say Glinda, I'm officially not speaking with you again."

Finn's face fell just a little. "None of them," she said. "Rehearsals are at the same time as my new varsity practice schedule."

"Oh, right," Gigi said. "We won't have practice together anymore."

"But I'm going to come to all of your games," Finn said. "I promise."

"You really don't have to do that."

The girls were silent for a minute. Then Gigi said,

"It's just going to be so weird. We used to do everything together. Now it's like we're not doing *anything* together."

"I know what you mean," Finn said. "But you know what? It doesn't change the fact that you will always, *always* be my bestie. I mean, you're like my sister, Gee. We don't always need to be in the same place at the same time doing the *same exact thing* to be connected. Do we?"

As she said the words, Gigi could feel how much Finn meant them. They were true for her too. It was hard for her to let go of the way things had always been, but maybe that was just growing up. It didn't have to mean the end of the world.

Gigi pointed to the Wall. "I think it's time."

"Time?"

"To hit the reset button."

For the next half hour, Eff and Gee carefully took down each and every scrap of paper from the Wall. Gigi placed the pieces into two giant manila envelopes and gave one to Finn. "What came before was great, but we don't need to be tied down by the past. From now on, let's focus on being good friends to each other *right now* and making some new memories."

Finn nodded. "Sounds good. Long as I can still come over for our regular Saturday-night slumber parties."

"Uh, you better," Gigi joked. "Or I'll sic Fred the Freckle on you. He'll whisper words of guilt in your ear while you sleep."

"Deal," Finn said. She peeked in her envelope and pulled out the snapshot of the two of them on their first day of pre-K. "We need to make a new addition. Go get your camera."

Gigi handed it over to Finn. "What exactly are we adding?"

"A new one of these," Finley said, shaking the preschool photo at Gigi. "In celebration of the new us."

Finn put her arm around Gigi and crouched a little to be closer to her friend's height. Gigi had to stand on her toes to get their faces to line up.

They weren't the same height anymore, they weren't wearing the same clothes, and they didn't like all of the same things, either. But the one thing that hadn't changed—the one thing that would never, *ever* change, Gigi thought, was the love between them. Gigi knew that now. She wished she had believed in it all along.

Finn extended her arm, the camera's lens pointing towards them.

"Say it, Gee," Finn commanded.

Gigi said, "No, you first."

"We'll say it together. On the count of three."

One.

Two.

Three.

"Long live Eff and Gee!"

SNAP!

*TURN THE PAGE FOR A SNEAK PEEK
OF PICTURE PERFECT #3*

"And where exactly do you think you're going?" Alice's mom called out.

Alice tried to suppress a smile, her hand on the latch as she pretended to leave for school.

"The bus stop?" Alice said, all innocence, turning away from the side gate as her mother stood on the back stoop, fists on her hips in pretend sternness.

"Not so fast," Mrs. Kinney said, and then she and her daughter grinned at each other. Alice's mom held up a silver camera dangling from her wrist. The two of them had played this little first-day-of-school game since Alice was in kindergarten, when she had begun to march off to the bus stop before learning that a) Kinneys always took photos on the first day of school and b) kindergartners don't take the bus to school all by themselves. (Although freshly minted middle schoolers—which Alice was today—did!)

"Ready? Say cheese!" Mrs. Kinney said. Alice

slumped her shoulders over, crossed her eyes, and stuck out her tongue, first-day-of-school zombie style.

"That pose doesn't really scream 'honors student,'" Alice's dad said, stepping outside with his mug of coffee and his shirt cuffs unbuttoned. Alice smiled, rolled her eyes, stood up straight, and re-posed in a more traditional manner, shaking her long red hair so that it flowed over her shoulders. Her parents could be embarrassing, but sweet—they were so proud of her for getting into honors classes, but really, it wasn't that big a deal. It's not like Alice set out to get there. It just . . . happened. Alice heard the fake-shutter sound of the digital camera, but then her mom kept holding the camera up for a few extra moments after taking the picture.

"Everything okay?" Alice asked.

"Oh yeah," Mrs. Kinney said, and finally lowered the camera, emitting a tiny sniffle.

"Are you *crying*?" Alice asked in disbelief. "It's just school, Mom. I've done this before. School bus, pens, notebooks, teachers, remember?"

"I know," Mrs. Kinney said, laughing and running the side of her thumb below her lower eyelashes to collect any mascara that may have dripped. "It's just . . . five seconds ago you were off to kindergarten.

Now . . . middle school."

"*Honors* middle school," her dad said proudly, just as Alice heard the side gate latch. *Ugh*. Couldn't Cassidy have come at any other moment?

"Yes, *honors* middle school," Alice's best friend repeated teasingly, entering the Kinneys' back yard with her own mom behind her. Mr. and Mrs. Kinney beamed with pride, not realizing that there was the teensiest bit of tension between the two girls over this particular detail. Alice and Cassidy had been in the same class ever since the Turners had moved in across the street when the girls were five years old, but this year, while Alice had tested into honors, Cassidy . . . didn't. Alice knew Cassidy was supportive, but the whole thing still felt a little weird.

It wasn't that Cassidy wasn't smart: she had good grades and was funnier than Alice could ever hope to be. Alice just seemed to possess a little extra nerdiness when it came to school, and now, being separated from her best friend and being singled out in general for being "gifted" was her "reward."

Alice would have been just fine sticking with regular classes, especially since the honors thing had been a source of awkwardness between the two of them over the summer. While Alice said things like "I don't know how I'm going to make it without having you in my class! What if the other kids are mean? Or total dorks? Or worse, *totally mean dorks*?" Cassidy would say things like "Oh, you're *smart*, you'll figure it out," followed up by a hasty "I'm just kidding."

Alice knew, though, that they could move past it with just a bit of time. Being in separate classes just had to become the new normal. Alice needed Cassidy on her side the same way she knew Cassidy needed her, because middle school? Seemed a little scary.

"Cass, get over here," Alice said, yanking her friend over to pose in a first-day-of-school photo with her.

Cass patted the side of her head with her palm self-consciously. Over the summer she had made the very bold decision to cut off her shoulder-length braids and rock a short natural do. Her mom was thrilled.

"She said, 'Oh, honey, you look like me from the eighties!' and I swear she would have started crying a little bit if I didn't tell her to stop," Cass reported in her post-haircut debrief earlier that week. Of course, looking like your mom wasn't exactly at the top of the wish list of any self-respecting middle schooler.

However, with the haircut, Cass *did* look more confident, more sophisticated. Alice knew for a fact that the new do was going to be a sensation, just like everything Cassidy did. *Everyone* wanted to be Cassidy's friend, boys and girls alike, but only Alice could count her as her best friend.

"I remember the first time you girls met." Cassidy's mom started to reminisce for probably the third time that week. Getting misty about old times was one of Mrs. Turner's quirks that Alice adored, along with the never-ending supply of fire-flavored Jolly Ranchers in her purse and the zoomy little white convertible she drove, with the license plate that read HERS.

Mr. Turner was nice and all, but if Alice was going to get a ride home with Cassidy, she always hoped Mrs. Turner would show up in that convertible.

"Cassidy just toddled right up to Alice, who was playing in the front yard the day we moved in, and demanded, 'Let's be best friends,'" Mrs. Turner continued.

"Here she goes again," said Cassidy, rolling her eyes. Alice pretended to take a nap on her shoulder.

"And Alice said, 'Okay!'" Mrs. Kinney filled in. "'Okay!' Just like that."

"And you held hands and ran through the sprinkler together. It was the most beautiful thing. And now look at you: best friends through all these years," added Mrs. Turner.

"Stop, you're going to get me going again!" Mrs. Kinney said, flapping her hands in front of her face.

"Mom, can you *please* just take the picture?" Alice asked. She actually didn't mind the reminiscing, but she sensed an impatient twitch in the golden-brown shoulders she had her arm slung over. It was time to get a move on and take this plunge, together.

Together—but only sort of, a glum voice in Alice's voice said.

She couldn't help wondering whether Cassidy was, maybe, a little bit mad about her leaving the general track for honors. All summer long, Alice had tried to work up the courage to ask if she was okay about it. The last time she'd attempted to address it, she and Cass were picking their way across the beach near their house one late-summer evening. Lake Michigan was calmly lapping at their brightly painted toenails as the sun went down.

"So, with the honors class thing . . . ," Alice ventured. (Okay, so she was also an honors-level awkward conversationalist.)

Cassidy cut her off. "It's fine!" she said in the same bright-but-fake voice that Alice's mom used when she "wasn't mad" that Alice's dad hadn't put the laundry away. "We don't have to talk about it."

Alice clammed up, choosing to listen to Cassidy's words, even if she had a hard time ignoring her tone.

Now Mrs. Kinney snapped the photo and peered at the photo on the screen. "Another keeper!" she pronounced, and Alice smiled, although she wasn't surprised. She and Cassidy had plotted their first-day-of-school outfits the week before, making sure that they'd complement each other but not clash (or, heaven forbid, *match*). Alice wore a summery navy-and-white striped dress with a white jean jacket. It was already almost eighty degrees (North Shore summers lasted almost as long as its winters), but the air conditioning in the middle school, she had heard, could reach sub-arctic temperatures.

Cassidy, meanwhile, wore a bright red cardigan over a white T-shirt and black shorts with white polka dots on them. Alice would have looked like a little kid in them, but they showed off Cassidy's long, lean ballet-toned legs.

They agreed it would be okay if they both wore the gold sandals they had bought together earlier that summer, accented with fresh pedicures. Hey, even if they wouldn't spend every single second of school together, at least when they did, they'd look awesome together—best friends ready to take on a new adventure.

"I couldn't sleep last night," Alice confessed, once they were on the bus. Cassidy turned towards her, eyes squinting from the sunlight reflecting off the sparkling lake. "But while I was tossing and turning, I came up with a stupendous plan!" Cassidy raised her eyebrows in amusement as Alice rummaged through her new backpack. It was oatmeal colored, with a design on the pocket that looked like a panda's head, with cute dark brown ears and everything. Alice relished the relative emptiness of the bag, when all she had rolling around in there were her new notebooks and school supplies and lip gloss; she had a feeling by the end of the day it would feel a lot heavier.

"Here it is!" Alice pulled out a purple notebook triumphantly. It was the perfect medium size, not so small that you couldn't write anything real in it, but just a *little* smaller than a regular school notebook (so a busy girl could find it just by feeling inside her locker or backpack).

"A notebook? Gee, you shouldn't have." Cassidy grinned.

"No, see, this is how we're going to stay in touch," Alice said. "Since we can't be in class together, we can keep each other up-to-date on everything that happens.

Mean teachers, cute guys, gym embarrassments—everything!"

"I love it!" said Cassidy. "But do you think we'll have time for it? I mean, I'll have ballet and you'll be busy making Albert Einstein look like a chump."

"No, it'll be fun!" Alice said. "We don't have to write, like, *everything* down. Just fun little stories and jokes we hear and stuff. I'll give you my locker combination and you can give me yours and we'll drop it off to each other between classes. It'll be like getting mail!"

Cassidy laughed. "Of course I'll do it. You do love your mail."

When she was six, Alice had embarked upon a master plan for getting new pen pals. She intended to float helium balloons with her name and address and a request for a postcard attached to the balloon's string. She had visions of letters from Russia, Ghana, Indonesia—until her mother gently pointed out that the balloons were more likely to get stuck in the neighborhood trees or fall into the lake and strangle a duck. It turned out the only thing Alice loved more than getting mail was not feeling like a duck killer.

Gradually the bus filled up with kids. Cassidy and Alice excitedly greeted the friends they knew from Comiskey Elementary and subtly eyed the students who came from other schools. Some of the girls looked nice; some of the guys looked especially cute; one girl with long, flowing dark curls and a tiny rosebud mouth glared at the floor and stomped down the bus aisle as if she didn't want to be there. Like it or not, Cassidy and Alice would be in classes with *all* these new kids. Time would tell who would prove to be friend or foe.

"I feel like we already have a *lot* of material for the notebook," Cassidy whispered with a sly grin once the year's cast of characters had assembled. Alice beamed and scribbled a quick kickoff note to Cassidy.

Maybe this will all be okay despite the fact that I'm being sent to nerd purgatory. Which should actually be called nerdatory. Portmanteau, right? Ugh, this is why I'm such a nerd in the first place! Happy first day of school . . . gulp!

READY FOR A PICTURE-PERFECT

FRIENDSHIP?

Molly Larsen had an awesome life—a great best friend and a prime spot on her gymnastics squad—before her family moved. Now the only person in the Garden State Molly gets along with is her neighbor Shrimp. But Shrimp is about as far from popular as anyone can be.

What's a new girl have to do to get some friends around here?

HARPER
An Imprint of HarperCollinsPublishers

www.harpercollinschildrens.com